## "Who are you?"

She crossed her arms. "I'm Sabrina Gonzalez."

"The bookkeeper who's taken up residence in my mother's house."

"And you're the rude, arrogant man who called earlier, the one with no manners."

Jared had been accused of worse, but he didn't take any guff from anyone. Never had, never would.

And he didn't trust Sabrina Gonzalez any farther than he could throw her—something that wouldn't be too tough. She was just a slip of a thing, with a slinky veil of black hair that nearly reached her waist.

She was just over five feet tall. Her eyes, the color of a field of bluebonnets in the spring, were big and expressive. She had high cheekbones. Lips that were kissable in spite of the pretty pout she wore.

He wondered what her hard luck story had been.

Dear Reader,

Winter is coming to an end, and spring is nearly here. As I write this letter, I'm sitting in my office. A light rain is dancing upon my window, and a pot of chicken and rice soup is simmering on the stove. It's the perfect time to curl up with a good book.

I'm glad you chose to read *Romancing the Cowboy,* the first book in the TEXAS HOMECOMING series. In Brighton Valley, Texas, you'll meet Granny Clayton, a widow who adopted three lonely boys and offered them love and a home on her ranch. Now that the boys have grown up, it's time for them to settle down. And Granny has just the women in mind for her boys.

If you get a chance, please stop by my Web site to let me know what you think of this new series, and enter my special contest. One lucky reader will receive a six-month subscription to the Special Edition Book Club. There are other prizes, too. Winners will be announced on or around April 15, 2008.

In the meantime, happy reading!

*Judy*
www.JudyDuarte.com

# ROMANCING THE COWBOY

## *JUDY DUARTE*

Silhouette

**SPECIAL EDITION**

Published by Silhouette Books

**America's Publisher of Contemporary Romance**

SILHOUETTE BOOKS

®

ISBN-13: 978-0-373-24888-9
ISBN-10:    0-373-24888-1

ROMANCING THE COWBOY

**Books by Judy Duarte**

Silhouette Special Edition

*Cowboy Courage* #1458
*Family Practice* #1511
*Almost Perfect* #1540
*Big Sky Baby* #1563
*The Virgin's Makeover* #1593
*Bluegrass Baby* #1598
*The Rich Man's Son* #1634
*\*Hailey's Hero* #1659
*\*Their Secret Son* #1667
*\*\*Their Unexpected Family* #1676
*\*Worth Fighting For* #1684
*\*The Matchmakers' Daddy* #1689

*His Mother's Wedding* #1731
*Call Me Cowboy* #1743
*†The Perfect Wife* #1773
*Rock-A-Bye Rancher* #1784
*Daddy on Call* #1822
*The Cowboy's Lullaby* #1834
*†† Romancing the Cowboy* #1888

\*Bayside Bachelors
\*\*Montana Mavericks:
   Gold Rush Grooms
†Talk of the Neighborhood
††The Texas Homecoming

## JUDY DUARTE

always knew there was a book inside her, but since English was her least favorite subject in school, she never considered herself a writer. An avid reader who enjoys a happy ending, Judy couldn't shake the dream of creating a book of her own.

Her dream became a reality in March 2002 when the Silhouette Special Edition line released her first book, *Cowboy Courage*. Since then, she has sold nineteen more novels. In July 2005, Judy won a prestigious Reader's Choice Award for *The Rich Man's Son*.

Judy makes her home near the beach in Southern California. When she's not cooped up in her writing cave, she's spending time with her somewhat enormous but delightfully close family.

You can write to Judy c/o Silhouette Books, 233 Broadway, Suite 1001, New York, NY 10237. You can also contact her at JudyDuarte@sbcglobal.net or through her Web site, www.judyduarte.com.

To Colleen Holth, who has been my friend for almost as long as I can remember. Thanks for letting me rope you into just about anything. I love you, Col.

## Chapter One

"I need to talk to you about Edna." At the sound of Doc Graham's age-worn voice over the telephone line, Jared Clayton's gut clenched and his chest tightened. This, he suspected, was the moment he'd been dreading. The call he and his two brothers had known would someday come.

He'd been sitting in the worn, tufted-leather chair in his study, the ledger spread across the polished oak desktop, when the phone rang.

Edna Clayton, who was known as Granny to most folks in the small Texas community of Brighton Valley, had adopted Jared when he'd been a gangly adolescent. At the time, he'd had nowhere else to go except the county home for boys. And for the next twenty years, the elderly widow had been the only real mother he'd known.

Jared waited for the small-town physician to tell him

the reason he'd called. Instead, Doc asked, "How long has it been since you visited the ranch?"

"A year or so." Jared made of a point of spending the major holidays with her and whichever brother could make it, although he'd missed being home last Christmas, due to a crisis on his own ranch—a divorce that had caught him completely by surprise. "But I call regularly."

*Oh, yeah?* a small voice asked.

When was the last time he'd picked up the phone to chat with·her, to ask how things were going?

A couple of weeks, he suspected. Or maybe a month.

Guilt rode him hard. He hadn't meant to let it go that long. And the fact that he'd been so damn focused lately—first on his divorce, then on his seriously injured brother—didn't help. At this point, neither Jolene nor Matthew seemed to be a good enough excuse.

"When did you talk to her last?" Doc had been Granny's best friend for as long as Jared could remember, but this was the first time Jared had felt as if he'd been called on the carpet by the man. Or maybe it was his own guilt doing a number on him.

"I meant to give her a call this evening," he lied, thinking he ought to actually schedule the time on his calendar so this wouldn't ever happen again. He'd make a point of checking in with her weekly, if not daily.

"It's just as well that you haven't yet done so."

"Why? What happened?"

"At this point? Nothing, but her memory is failing, and she's been having some health problems."

"Like what?" At seventy-nine, any number of things could wear out or go haywire. Maybe Jared ought to bring her to his ranch to live with him so he could keep an eye on her, but she'd always been so independent and set in her ways. And the old Granny, the one who'd raised him, would never agree. He'd have to hog-tie her and throw her over his shoulder in order to convince her to leave the Rocking C, the only home she'd had in nearly sixty years.

"I can't seem to control her blood pressure," Doc said, "even with medication. She has a heart murmur, and I'm afraid she may not have much time left."

A stab of grief shot through him, stirring up his memories—the *good* ones. Granny and his adopted brothers, Matt and Greg, were the only family he'd ever really had.

"Since I doubt Edna will let you boys know what's going on, I thought I'd better call."

Jared couldn't help thinking that Granny's heart had worn out over the years. The idea wasn't founded upon medical science by any means, but it seemed as though all the good deeds and charity work she'd done over the course of her life had finally taken their toll.

For as long as folks in Brighton Valley had known her, Granny had been taking in strays of all shapes and sizes— human ones, as well as the four-legged variety. And Jared thanked his lucky stars that he'd been one of them.

He had his own spread now, nearly a hundred miles away, but that didn't mean he didn't love her dearly. Granny was the only woman who had always come through for him and never let him down—one way or another.

"Give it to me straight, Doc."

"Well, I think she needs to go into Houston and see a cardiologist, but I've never seen a woman so dang stubborn in all my life." Since Doc had attended the local high school with Edna and was pushing eighty himself, that was saying a lot.

"Is she all right living out on that ranch alone?" Jared asked, thinking that they might need to hire a nurse to look after her if he couldn't talk her in to moving in with him.

"She's *not* alone," Doc said. "That's another issue completely. Right now, she's got a full house."

"What do you mean?" The last time Jared had gone by the ranch, the only ones living there had been Granny and Lester Bailey, the foreman, plus a couple of newly hired greenhorns who tried hard but didn't know much about cattle. Thank goodness the other hands knew what to do without being told. "Who's she taken in now?"

"A whole passel of women, one of whom looked pregnant to me. And there's at least one kid."

Oh, for Pete's sake. Jared, of all people, ought to be understanding of Granny's hospitality. But she was getting older now and was more vulnerable than she'd been in the past.

"Looks like I'd better make a trip south tomorrow." Of course, he'd have to find someone to look after Matthew. Jared had a bad feeling about leaving him alone, especially in his present frame of mind.

"You probably ought to consider staying at Edna's for a while," Doc added.

"Why is that?"

"I spoke to Grant Whitaker about her yesterday when we were eating breakfast down at Caroline's Diner."

Grant was Granny's CPA, at least he had been. He

had to be Granny and Doc's age. Or at least getting close. "Hasn't he retired yet?"

"Nope. He still works for Edna and a couple other longtime clients. And he was concerned about something. He decided to run it by me first, before bothering you boys with it."

Jared stiffened. "What was he worried about?"

"Grant seems to think there's a discrepancy in her accounts."

"What *kind* of discrepancy?" Jared asked.

"He says there have been a significant number of electronic withdrawals over the past few weeks."

"I don't know how in the hell that could have happened. Granny doesn't even have a computer."

"Apparently, she does now. Her new bookkeeper talked her into getting one."

She hired a new bookkeeper? One who had access to online banking, account numbers and passwords? Jared gripped the receiver until he thought he might choke the truth out of it. "I'm not going to wait until morning. I'll give her a call now and tell her… Hell, I'll think of something. Either way, I'm leaving this evening."

"Good. If she were my mother, I'd want to know."

"If someone *is* taking advantage of her, they'll wish they weren't."

"Now, don't go in there half-cocked, son. There could be a logical explanation for all of this."

Yeah. Right.

Granny needed him.

And now it was his turn to be there for her.

As he disconnected the line, a flash of lightning

briefly illuminated the oak-paneled study. He pushed himself away from the desk, then strode to the open window in slow steady steps as a rumble of thunder rolled across the evening sky.

The scent of rain mingled with smoke from the chimney. He could smell the storm coming. For a moment, he considered waiting it out and driving after it passed, but he didn't think on it too long.

He needed to get to Granny's ranch and find out what he was up against. He shut the window, then glanced at the clock on the bookshelf. 8:38 p.m. It would be late by the time he and Matt arrived.

Jared had a key to the back door, but he didn't want to let himself in without telling Granny he was coming. So he dialed her number.

"Hello?" a woman answered, her voice laced with a slight Latina accent, her tone soft and gentle.

All the frustration and worry that had been swirling inside caused Jared to snap in a manner that was more sharp and brusque than usual. "Who are you?"

She paused momentarily. "Why don't you introduce yourself first?"

Patience had never been one of his virtues, not when he wanted answers. "In case you didn't hear me the first time, who the hell are you?"

She cleared her throat, yet the softness remained. "I'm Sabrina. I work here."

"Let me talk to Mrs. Clayton."

"I'm not sure I want you to."

"Excuse me?" His voice, rock hard and determined, mocked her velvety tone.

"She's resting, and I'd rather not see her upset."

Jared didn't know who this woman was, but he didn't like her already. "Why in blazes would I call to stir her up?"

"You seem to be irritated about something, sir. And I can't see any point in raising her blood pressure."

"Listen here, Sabrina. *You're* raising *my* blood pressure. All I want to do is talk to Edna, to ask how she's feeling, to check on her."

She remained silent for the longest time, as if trying to determine whether she was talking to a friend or a foe.

"This is Jared," he said, although she didn't respond right away.

Hadn't Granny even told those women about him? About how she'd adopted not only Jared, but also two other boys, who loved her and would do anything to protect her?

Apparently not.

The memory lapses Doc had mentioned came to mind, and Jared was even more determined to set things right. Even if it meant backpedaling and reining in a conversation that he now realized had started off on a bad foot.

"Maybe we ought to slow down a bit and clear the air. I'm Edna's oldest son. And I'd like to talk to her. I get a little riled up when someone tries to put me off."

"She told me about you. I'm sorry. I'll get her."

When the woman set down the receiver, silence filled the line. A barrage of questions begged for answers. And not just questions about Granny's health, the women who'd infiltrated the ranch and the loss of money in Granny's account.

What had Granny said about Jared?

It could have been any number of things, he supposed. But sometimes Granny had a way of revealing secrets, things a guy would rather keep to himself. And her lack of discretion was one reason he hadn't gone into details about the divorce with her, just the irreconcilable differences part.

The *real* reason Jolene had left him remained deeply hidden within a ragged crevice in his heart.

"Jared?" that familiar, maternal voice asked. "Is that you?"

"Yes, Granny. How are you doing?"

"Fine as frog's hair," she responded. Then she made a fruitless attempt to cover the mouthpiece of the phone and speak to someone else, most likely Sabrina. "Thank you, dear. No, I'll lock up for the night. Go on to bed."

"Granny?" he asked, a bit put out that she'd be chatting with one of the moochers instead of him.

"I'm sorry. Where were we?" Granny asked.

"I asked how you were doing."

"Oh, yes. I'm doing just fine. How about you? Are you well?"

Jared had been doing okay until Matthew moved in. And until Doc had called this evening. "I'm all right. Keeping busy."

"What about Matt?" Granny said. "Is he doing okay, too?"

"Yes," Jared said, not wanting to worry his mother. But the truth was, although Matt seemed to be mending physically, he'd been depressed ever since the accident.

Of course, Jared really couldn't blame him. Matt had been the driver in the accident that killed his fiancée and her son. And he'd been the only one in the vehicle to survive.

"Does he still have to use a wheelchair?"

"Yes, but hopefully that's only temporary." Jared had built ramps to help him get in and out of the house, even though he seemed to prefer being inside. Or near the liquor cabinet.

"I'm sure it's tough on him," Granny said. "A man like Matt doesn't cotton to being laid up."

Jared wouldn't like it, either. And while he wasn't sure what Matt would say about the decision to go back to the Rocking C for a few days, he thought it might do him some good.

"You don't usually call so late," Granny said. "Is there something wrong?"

He suspected so, which was why he decided to lie about his reason for going back to the ranch and staying for a few days. "Matt and I have a couple of business meetings in Houston over the next week or so. We thought we'd come down, stay with you and drive back and forth."

"Why, of course. I'll ask Tori to make up beds in the den and in the guestroom."

"Who's Tori?"

"My new maid."

"Then who is Sabrina?" he asked.

"She's my new bookkeeper."

Aw. The suspected thief. "What's she doing at your house this late?"

"She and her nephew live here."

The hordes had begun to move in, ready to pounce and take advantage of one of the kindest little old ladies in Texas. And Jared wasn't going to let that happen.

"I guess I'll meet her when we get there."

"When are you coming?" she asked.

"Late tonight. But don't wait up. I've got a key."

And once Jared got to Granny's ranch, he was going to take control of a sorry situation, evict a few freeloaders and see to it the thief ended up in jail.

It was after midnight, but Sabrina Gonzalez had never been able to sleep very well in an unfamiliar house. So it was no wonder she was wide-awake on one of the twin-size beds in the small guestroom Mrs. Clayton had given her to share with Joey. Her new job, which had been a blessing in and of itself, came with room and board, too. That was a bit out of the ordinary for a bookkeeper, but Sabrina wasn't about to complain.

Besides, the room inside the Clayton ranch house was only temporary, since Mrs. Clayton planned to remodel an old cabin on the grounds. Sabrina and Joey, her six-year-old nephew, would move in as soon as it was ready for them. But God only knew how long that would be. The rustic structure hadn't been used in ages, so it would need a lot of work to be livable.

Sabrina stopped by Joey's bedside and gently caressed the top of his head.

Carlos, her twin brother and Joey's dad, had been convicted of a crime he hadn't committed and was currently serving time in prison, so Sabrina had stepped in as a guardian.

At first, when Mrs. Clayton's job offer came through, Sabrina had declined to take it, since the ranch was quite a drive from Houston and she hadn't found a competent and trustworthy sitter for her nephew yet. But the elderly woman had invited both Sabrina and Joey to live at the ranch, insisting that it was best for the motherless boy to be near a loved one at a time like this and not in day care.

How could Sabrina argue with that?

Joey stirred, and she shushed him until he grew still. Before leaving the room, she stopped by the closet for a robe, then hesitated. The door squeaked terribly when it slid open, and she hated to make any unnecessary noise.

Besides, what would it hurt to walk out into the kitchen wearing just her nightgown? There were only women in the house.

A night-light lit her way downstairs, the steps creaking under her weight. She walked into the living room, where she flipped on a lamp, illuminating the room. Then she went to the kitchen.

Connie, the new cook, was a sweetheart, but she hadn't been hired for her culinary skills. The oatmeal cookies she'd made, however, were the best Sabrina had ever tasted.

Rather than turn on every light in the house, Sabrina decided not to flip on the switch. She could make her way through the dimly lit kitchen easy enough.

She opened the fridge and poured herself a glass of milk, just as a car engine sounded outside. She glanced at the clock. 12:17 a.m. Surely, Edna wasn't expecting company. Maybe someone on the highway had made a wrong turn and was lost. The driver would figure it out soon enough, she supposed, and head back to the road.

She plucked two of the chewy cookies from the plastic container in which Connie had stored them and wrapped them in a paper towel to take into the living room, where she would eat them as she thumbed through a magazine.

But the vehicle didn't turn around or back out. Instead, the engine continued to idle, and the headlights remained on.

A door opened and shut.

When Sabrina heard a baritone whisper through a window that had been left partially open, she froze. Another voice responded, this one a bit louder.

One of the hired hands?

Maybe so.

She pinched off a bite of one cookie and popped it into her mouth, relishing the taste of raisins and spice, then took a sip of milk.

More voices—all male—sounded. Another door opened, then shut.

"Be quiet," a man said, as he neared the window. "I don't want to wake up anyone in the house."

"I hate this," another added.

"We don't like it, either. Just sit back and enjoy the ride, kid."

Footsteps sounded at the back porch. It might be the end of spring, but a winter frost crept up Sabrina's spine. Her heart pounded out an ominous dirge in her brain and perspiration beaded on her forehead.

As quiet as a cornered mouse, she tiptoed toward the kitchen counter, where the butcher block rested. She set down her milk and cookies, then grabbed the biggest weapon she could find—a meat cleaver—and held it with both hands, ready to defend herself.

Maybe it was Lester, the ranch foreman, and some of the hired hands. Maybe they had reason to be awake and milling about at this time of night.

That had to be it, yet her pulse escalated until she

could hear it throbbing in her ears. An avid mystery reader with a wild imagination, Sabrina often thought in terms of worst-possible scenarios. And she tried to keep that in mind, tried to remain calm.

She could scream, waking everyone in the house. And what if there was a perfectly good explanation for all of this?

Then the new ranch bookkeeper would look like a fool.

The lock clicked, as though someone had a key. Or perhaps someone was picking it.

Should she scream now?

The door to the mudroom swung open, revealing a group of men outside, their forms barely illuminated by the headlights of a vehicle. The one in front, a tall, thirty-something hulk of a man with wheat-colored hair, held a key in his hand and gaped at her. "Who the hell are you?"

If she'd witnessed a crime and stood behind a mirrored window, looking at a lineup and listening to each voice, she'd recognize *that* one.

Jared Clayton.

She didn't know whether to cry in relief or anger. "Didn't anyone teach you to knock on doors?"

"Not at *this* house."

"Hey," a voice behind him said, "get a move on. This is heavy."

Jared stepped aside, and several of the ranch hands carried a dark-haired man and the wheelchair in which he was still seated through the service porch and into the kitchen, where they lowered him to the floor.

"I'm sorry," she said, more in response to the injured man's plight than anything.

From what she'd heard, the one-time rodeo cowboy

had been involved in a tragic car accident a while back, and he'd been recuperating at Jared's ranch. Yet her gaze and her focus turned to Jared. "You scared me."

"Oh, yeah?" Jared's features—quite handsome in the light—softened a tad. "And you don't think seeing a she-devil, wielding a meat cleaver in her hand and dressed like a ghost in flowing white didn't give me a start, too?"

Sabrina glanced down at her gown, realizing how threadbare the fabric had become, how sheer the material.

Her hair hung down her back, but she freed the side tresses, allowing them to cover the front of her gown the best they could.

As Matthew wheeled himself out of the kitchen and into the living room, the ranch hands backed out the door, closing it and leaving her with Mrs. Clayton's oldest son. He still hadn't formally introduced himself, although he really hadn't needed to.

He crossed his arms across a broad chest and shifted the bulk of his weight to one, denim-clad hip. "Who are *you?*"

She crossed her own arms, hoping that would help hide what her hair couldn't. "I'm Sabrina Gonzalez."

"The bookkeeper who's taken up residence in my mother's house."

It wasn't a question, yet his tone, his condescension, set her off, provoking a retort that was completely out of character. "And you're the rude, arrogant man who called earlier."

Jared had been accused of worse, but he didn't take any guff off anyone. Never had, never would.

Granny had done her best to teach him and his brothers to be cordial and polite, but it didn't come easy to Jared. Not when he had reason to believe someone was a liar or a cheat. And he didn't trust Sabrina Gonzalez any farther than he could throw her—something that wouldn't be too tough. She was just a slip of a thing, with a slinky veil of black hair that nearly reached her waist.

Jared, who'd always favored long-haired women, found it intriguing. Attractive.

But he didn't dare give this particular woman more than a passing glance. She was, after all, the one with the easiest access to Granny's accounts. And it didn't take much skill to put two and two together. He could do the math on that.

"Are you going to put down your weapon?" he asked.

She glanced at the cleaver, then replaced it into the butcher-block holder. Turning to face him again and re-crossing her arms, she gave a little shrug. "The ranch is off the beaten path, and I wasn't sure if this was a home invasion."

"My guess is that you watch too much television."

Her eyes, the color of a field of bluebonnets in the spring, were big and expressive. Her lashes, thick and dark, didn't need mascara.

She was a beautiful woman, even without makeup and dressed in an old gown. Of course, her bedtime attire and sleep-tousled hair had an appeal in and of itself.

To much of one, he decided.

He knew better than to allow himself to be swayed by lust and did his best to shake off any sexual interest in her.

"So what were you doing awake and prowling around in the house at this hour?" he asked

She paused, as if deciding whether to tell the truth or to lie. "Sometimes I have trouble falling asleep, so I came for a glass of milk."

"You might try whiskey. It works for me."

The hands that she'd tucked under her arms loosened, leaving him a glimpse of the gentle swell of her breasts.

Her white cotton gown had seen better days, but her body was damn near perfect. What he could see of it, anyway.

He pulled out a chair from the antique oak table, took a seat and studied her.

Early twenties. Just over five feet tall. High cheekbones, big eyes. Lips that were kissable in spite of the pretty pout she wore.

He wondered what her hard-luck story had been. "So how'd you meet Granny?"

She remained standing. "I was referred by Mr. Whitaker, and I came out to the ranch for an interview."

Grant referred her? If so, that was interesting. Grant had been the one to pick up on the discrepancies in the account.

"I'd originally applied for work at his office," she added, "but he's cutting back on his workload. He knew Mrs. Clayton needed a bookkeeper, so he gave her a call."

By the way she tried to cover herself, Jared suspected she was embarrassed to be standing before him in her nightgown, but apparently she was too proud to make excuses and flee.

And he was too ornery to give her a reason to leave.

Besides, he had some questions to ask her.

That is, until a young, sleepy voice sounded in the doorway of the kitchen. "Aunt Sabrina?"

The woman turned to where a small, dark-haired boy of about five or six stood, rubbing his eyes.

She crossed the distance between them, placing her

hand upon his shoulder. "It's okay, Joey. I'm sorry the men woke you. Why don't you go back to bed? I'll be there in a minute."

"I was worried 'bout you," he said. "Worried you left me here and wouldn't come back."

She stooped, her gown pooling onto the kitchen floor. She wrapped her arms around the boy. "I'd never leave you, Joey. Not on purpose."

"But my mommy…"

"I know, honey. But that wasn't on purpose."

Jared raked a hand through his hair. He wasn't sure what that was all about. But it sounded like the hint of a hard-luck story to him, and knowing Granny, she'd been more swayed by Sabrina's tale of woe than her qualifications, resume or references.

"Come on," Sabrina told the boy. "I'll walk you back to the bedroom."

As she ushered Joey through the doorway, her hair covered most of her back, swaying with her steps. But the thin material of her nightgown did little to hide her shapely hips.

Jared suspected she wasn't aware that the light was playing a trick on her, baring a slight outline of the panties she wore. Something decent and conservative. A pair worthy of any churchgoing matron.

Yet on Sabrina, with her ebony hair flirting with the elastic waistband, they fit her bottom in a way that would tempt a saint. And Jared was far from saintly.

Especially when he was determined to uncover a liar and a thief.

## Chapter Two

On most nights, when those dreaded bouts of insomnia struck, Sabrina would finally fall asleep just before dawn, only to find it hard to wake up when it was time to begin the next day.

But that wasn't the case this morning.

After having had the liver scared out of her by Jared Clayton and his entourage last night, she hadn't been able to sleep at all. Of course, as much as she'd like to blame that on his unannounced arrival, it had been the tone of his voice and the implication in his words that had set her emotions on edge. He'd talked to her as though she were some kind of imposter or second-class citizen.

Standing in the kitchen, with his hands slapped onto his hips, golden-brown eyes narrowed with suspicion, square jaw lifted in challenge, he'd been a formidable opponent. And if he hadn't struck such an intimidating pose, she might have found the blond-haired rancher handsome.

Okay. So she'd found him handsome anyway. That didn't make him particularly appealing. Not to her. The kind of man she wanted for herself was caring and gentle, someone who pondered a situation before barking out commands or making rash judgments and snide comments.

Someone not at all like her employer's oldest son.

Sabrina's thoughts turned to the day she'd first arrived at the ranch. When Mrs. Clayton had given her a tour of the house, they'd stopped near the rustic stone fireplace in the spacious living room, where Sabrina had gravitated toward a hodgepodge of silver-framed photos gracing the mantel. When she had a family and a home of her own, she would display photographs, too.

One picture in particular piqued her curiosity, and she'd reached for the pewter frame of a young boy mounted on a black horse. His eyes fairly glistened with joy and a smile dimpled his cheeks.

"That's Jared the day he went out with the men for the very first time," the elderly woman had told Sabrina. "He was *so* proud. His early years had been spent in the city, so he had to learn to rope and ride first, but he was a natural. You would've thought he'd been born in a saddle."

Grant Whitaker, the elderly CPA who'd passed Sabrina's resume on to Mrs. Clayton, had mentioned something about the three boys the woman had adopted, all of whom had been down-and-out youngsters with nowhere else to go.

As Sabrina had studied the happy young boy in the photo, she'd been curious about his background. But since she'd always been one to keep her own…humble beginnings to herself, she didn't prod for any more information than her employer wanted to share.

"Jared's the oldest of my three sons," Mrs. Clayton had said. "He's grown up to be the kind of man a woman can depend upon. I suppose some would say he's loyal to a fault."

For a moment, Sabrina had wondered if the elderly woman had been trying her hand at matchmaking, but decided she was probably talking in a mother/son or family sense. Jared had certainly seemed to be looking out for his mother last night—if you could call a rabid dog protective.

Of course, he might have had good reason for being in a foul mood, like an abscessed tooth or a migraine headache. Still, try as she might, Sabrina couldn't imagine that scowling, brash man to be the same smiling boy she'd seen in the picture on the mantel.

As Sabrina had returned the frame to its rightful place, Mrs. Clayton had added, "Jared's a good boy. Of course, all my sons are."

That hadn't always been the case, though. From what Sabrina had heard in town, Edna "Granny" Clayton had opened her heart to people in need over the years, and no one had needed a home—or a firm hand—more than the three boys she'd adopted. Yet her generosity and kindness hadn't stopped there.

In the past few weeks, she'd not only taken in Sabrina and Joey, but she'd given Tori McKenzie and Connie Montoya jobs and a place to live, too. So now that Jared and his brother had arrived, the house was bursting at the seams. Of course, the living situation would improve once the cabin was renovated and one of the outbuildings was converted into two small apartments for the household staff.

Sabrina didn't know about the other two women, but she was really looking forward to the move.

As a child, she and her family had been forced to live with various relatives and she'd grown to hate feeling like a charity case. All she wanted was to have a home of her own, a place no one could ever take away from her, but she would be content with what she had now and do her best to create a stable environment for her nephew.

She plumped her pillow for the umpteenth time in the last hour or so, then rolled to the side of the bed and glanced across the room to where Joey slept. She was able to see his blanketed form without having to turn on the light, which meant morning had arrived, so she climbed from bed.

Before heading to the bathroom, she stopped at the window, drew open the white eyelet curtains and peered out at the grassy pasture where several horses grazed, then over to the big white barn. Near the double doors, some of the hired hands had begun to gather.

The Rocking C wasn't anything like the home she'd imagined having in the city, but Joey seemed to like it here, which was all that really mattered.

She let the curtains fall back into place and made her way to the shower. She was glad her room had a private bathroom she only had to share with Joey. She turned on the spigot, waiting until the water was the right temperature, then stepped inside. When she was done, she wrapped a towel around her and blow-dried her hair. Then she dressed in a pair of khaki slacks, a neatly pressed white cotton blouse and a black sweater.

Just months ago, she'd dreamed of living in the city and wearing business suits to work—a dream she would have to put on hold until Joey was older.

Still, she'd tried to dress the part of a professional on her first day at the Rocking C by wearing a skirt and blazer.

"Well, now, don't you look nice," Granny had said. "But dressing up all fancy isn't necessary around here."

Sabrina had glanced down at her outfit, then at the elderly woman who'd hired her. "I suppose this is a bit over the top for a bookkeeping position at a ranch, but I wanted to let you know I take this job seriously."

"I'm glad to hear it. But you'll be a lot more comfortable around here in denim and flannel."

Sabrina hadn't been able to go that far, so slacks and blouses had been a compromise. And even though Granny had purchased several pairs of jeans and some feminine-cut T-shirts as a surprise, Sabrina hadn't been able to wear them. Not for work.

Now ready to face the day, she took one last peek at her nephew, then quietly let herself out of the bedroom and started down the hall. The rich aroma of fresh-brewed coffee wafted through the sprawling, five-bedroom ranch house, letting her know she wasn't the first one up and moving about. A cupboard door opened and closed in the kitchen, suggesting that Connie had started to prepare breakfast. Sabrina wondered if the new cook had any idea there would be two more joining them for the morning meal—Jared and Matthew.

She supposed it didn't matter. Connie tried hard, and although her meals weren't anything to shout about, she usually prepared enough to feed an army.

Sabrina wasn't much of a breakfast eater herself, especially when she'd had a midnight snack. But last night she'd only had two cookies. If Jared hadn't shown up, she might have gone back for more, but she hadn't wanted to leave her room.

Before she could get three steps down the hall, she heard papers being shuffled in the dark-paneled, masculine office and stiffened. She'd become somewhat territorial about the room in which she worked. With Edna's permission, she'd spent the better part of two days arranging the furniture and setting up a filing system that suited her.

More paper shuffled and a drawer slid open.

Was Edna looking for something she'd misplaced again?

As Sabrina approached the open doorway, she spotted Jared seated at the desk, rifling through one of the drawers. Several open files lay across the scarred oak desktop.

"Looking for something?" she asked.

The rugged rancher glanced up. For one fleeting moment, he donned the expression of a boy who'd been caught with his hand in the church offering plate, but he quickly doused it.

Straightening, he leaned back in the seat, the leather and springs creaking from the shift in his weight. "Nope. Nothing in particular."

In that case, he'd been snooping, which she didn't appreciate one bit.

She crossed her arms and leaned against the door-jamb. "The office was a mess when I came to work, so I've organized it. I know exactly where everything is and can put my hands on it instantly. So if you ever decide what it is you need, just let me know. I'd be glad to get it for you."

His gaze traveled the length of her and back, as though he was trying to assess her—body and soul. A glimmer of masculine interest flashed in his eyes, and it was all she could do to remain ramrod straight. Calm. In control. She was determined to keep her pulse rate steady and her temper on an even keel.

"It's obvious that you've made a lot of changes," he said. "Granny used to file things in piles and stacks."

"I can't work like that."

"Ah, so you're a control freak."

She tensed. Over the years, she'd taken some ribbing because of her need to take charge of her life, but she couldn't help it. "I prefer to think of myself as organized."

He rocked back in the chair, causing it to strain and groan. "Where did you meet Grant Whitaker?"

Sabrina didn't like the idea of being interrogated and had the urge to tell Jared where he could get off. But she'd worked hard in college, choosing to bypass student loans and financial aid for reasons of her own, and didn't want him or anyone else to think of her as a charity case. Not anymore.

"I was majoring in accounting at the University of Houston and met Mr. Whitaker while applying for a job in his office. He wasn't hiring, but suggested I call Mrs.

Clayton, since she'd recently told him she was looking for a bookkeeper. I needed the job, and she needed me. It's as simple as that." She strode toward the desk. "While I don't usually waste my time speaking to rude, obnoxious people, you're my employer's son, so I'm trying to be polite. But I don't owe you anything, Mr. Clayton. Least of all an explanation."

A grin tugged at his lips, and a hint of—amusement? Admiration?—lit the gold flecks in his eyes. "I thought accountants were supposed to be mild-mannered. You've got a little spunk."

A part of her felt compelled to thank him, but she kept quiet.

"I suppose I've been…snappy," he admitted, "so I apologize. But there are a lot of people living here, all of them strangers, and I just want to make sure no one is taking advantage of Granny."

"Your mother strikes me as being a good judge of character."

"She always used to be."

Sabrina glanced at the files on the desk and eased closer so she could see what he'd been reading. "For someone who claims he isn't looking for anything, you sure have dug through quite a few files."

"Actually," he said, "I'm the executor of Granny's estate and I always go over the books when I'm in town."

"She didn't say anything to me about that."

"It probably slipped her mind."

That was certainly possible, Sabrina supposed. "Then maybe it's a good idea if we talk to her about it at break-fast. I'd feel much better if she gave me her okay."

Instead of responding to her comment, he studied

her. His hazel eyes, were compelling when they weren't narrowed or fired-up in anger. Mesmerizing, actually, so she broke eye contact.

About the time she assumed he wasn't going to respond at all, he said, "Your hair looks better down. Like you wore it last night."

The compliment, as well as the masculine appreciation in his tone, knocked her off balance, and she lifted her hand to feel along the side of her hair. Making sure the strands were in place, she supposed.

He cleared his throat. "Anyway, you don't need to worry. I'll put everything back where I found it."

"That's all right." Sabrina reached for a file, intending to gather them all together and make sure they ended up in the right place. "I'll do it."

Jared's hand clamped on to her wrist, and a jolt of heat shot straight through her chest, nearly taking her breath away. Time stood still, as sexual awareness hovered over her, unbalancing her.

She yanked free of his grip, a knee-jerk response that was more from the shocking zing of his touch than from being restrained.

Her parents had allowed themselves to be ruled by hormones instead of good sense. And look where that had gotten them.

Sabrina was determined not to make the same mistake, especially when she could clearly see that Jared Clayton wasn't the man for her.

"I'm not finished looking at those." As he withdrew his hand, his gaze softened ever so slightly.

"I have no problem allowing you to have the run of the office. But only if Mrs. Clayton gives her okay."

He leaned back in the chair, the leather and springs protesting again. Another grin eased across his lips, causing the warrior in him to relax some. "I value honesty, integrity and a good work ethic, Sabrina. So I hope that's what's going on here."

That's exactly what was going on. But the way he studied her made her wonder if he thought she had some kind of ulterior motive.

"Maybe we've started out on the wrong foot," he said, his eyes gentling even more.

He was right, but it wasn't Sabrina who'd set the ground rules. "I'm sure your mother would prefer that we be allies rather than adversaries."

"Is it too late to start over?"

She wanted to tell him it was. To insist the two of them might never see eye to eye.

Yet as her their gazes locked, as her heart rate slipped into overdrive, she wasn't so sure.

Jared hadn't been able to find anything suspicious in the office, so just before seven, he stopped by the kitchen to share a cup of coffee with the men who were downing the last bit of their breakfast—overcooked strips of bacon and misshapen, unevenly browned pancakes. Since Connie, the so-called cook, was nowhere to be seen, Jared suspected that she'd had been too embarrassed to stick around and witness the consumption of the meal.

But rather than hang out with the men any longer, Jared made small talk while he finished his coffee, then excused himself to check on his brother.

It was rare that Jared ever felt as though he was in

over his head, but in this case, with three women to question, as well as some of the ranch hands—if he could ever get them alone—he could use Matt's help.

His brother's bedroom door was closed, so he knocked lightly.

"Who is it?" Matt asked.

"It's me."

"Come on in."

Jared opened the door and entered the room. Matt was seated in his wheelchair. His dark brown hair was a tousled mess and he hadn't shaved in days. What most people might not know was that Matt's spirit had been more broken than his body.

"Want me to help you take a shower?" Jared asked.

"Maybe later." Matt nodded his head toward the office door. "Find out anything?"

"Not yet, but I haven't been able to go back too far. If worse comes to worst, I'll give Grant Whitaker a call."

"What are you going to do if you find out who's been tinkering with Granny's accounts?"

"Press charges for a start."

Last night, after Doc had called, Jared had given his brother the news. He'd hoped hearing about Granny's failing health and the missing funds might pull Matt out of the slump he'd been in ever since the accident.

"You have to come with me," he'd told his brother last night. "I'm going to need help convincing Granny to sell her place and move in with me."

But if truth be told, Jared had feared leaving Matt alone in his condition. No telling what he might do, even if he'd never made any outright threats to end it all.

Why else would he refuse to go to physical therapy?

If Jared had been the one laid low by shattered bones, he'd be champing at the bit to get better and back on his feet.

Now he was hoping that Matt's love for Granny would pull him out of the depression that threatened to keep him in that damn chair for the rest of his life.

"I need your help," he told Matt.

"What kind of help?"

In the past, Matt had always been just as protective and vigilant about the ranch and their mother's well-being as Jared was, but believing he'd caused the accident that killed his fiancée and her son had crippled him worse than the injuries he'd suffered that fateful night.

"I need you to keep your eyes and ears open. One of the strays Granny took in is a thief, and I'm not sure which one."

"What about the new bookkeeper?" Matt asked. "She has access to the bank accounts. Have you questioned her yet?"

"I wanted to do some poking around first." A small part of him hoped the lovely, dark-haired beauty with the skill and the opportunity to rob Granny blind was every bit as ethical and efficient as she claimed to be, although he couldn't say why. Someone was responsible for the missing funds, and heaven help whoever it was.

"Come on." Jared stepped behind Matt's wheelchair and began to push him out of the bedroom. "Let's go have breakfast, although I gotta tell you it smells much better than it looks. I just hope it tastes okay. When I was in there earlier, I didn't see any of the ranch hands go for seconds."

As Jared and Matt entered the hall, they blocked the

way of a tall, shapely redhead, who jerked back and gasped in surprise.

Jared opened his mouth to ask which of the freeloaders she was, but having already bumped heads with Sabrina, he decided to exercise a little more diplomacy this time. "We haven't met. I'm Jared Clayton, Granny's son, and this is Matthew, my brother."

"Tori McKenzie. The new housekeeper." Her gaze slid toward Matt, and curiosity played out on her face.

To her credit, she didn't ask any questions, which Matt probably appreciated. He didn't like talking about the car accident that had also ended his rodeo career.

"It's nice to meet you," Tori said.

"Same here." Jared forced a grin, yet doubted his brother made the same attempt. Matt didn't find much to smile about these days.

Tori stepped aside by entering the open doorway to the bathroom, allowing room for Matt's wheelchair to pass, and Jared continued on his way to the kitchen.

"Well, now," Granny said from her chair at the antique walnut table that had been in her family for years. "Isn't this a treat? All we're missing is Greg."

The youngest of the three boys, Greg, had always been in the limelight, first as a star football player in college and now as a country-and-western singer.

"Greg's on tour this month," Jared said.

After Doc's phone call last night, Jared had called his youngest brother, who was ready to cancel whatever shows necessary to come home, but Jared told him to hold off and that they'd keep him posted on the situation.

"Greg's getting pretty popular," Granny said.

"That's true, but the last time we talked, he mentioned wanting to come home for a visit as soon as he could swing it. I have a feeling he's going to surprise you one of these days soon." Jared didn't mention that the conversation had taken place last night.

The back door opened and shut, then a petite woman with short blond hair entered through the mudroom. She was attractive, Jared supposed, although he'd always been partial to brunettes.

Especially those with long dark hair—like Sabrina, he realized, although that was one attraction that wasn't going anywhere.

"Can I freshen anyone's coffee?" the blonde asked, as she headed to the sink and turned on the water to wash her hands.

Granny lifted her cup. "I'll have a tad more. And now that you're here, let me introduce you to my sons, Jared and Matt. Boys, this is Consuela Montoya. But she wants to be called Connie."

"It's nice to meet you." The woman smiled shyly, then reached for the coffeepot and replenished Granny's cup. "Anyone else?"

"Not yet," Matt said.

"I'll pass." Jared studied the woman, noting that her hair had been dyed. Had she been a brunette who'd come in to some cash lately?

Highlights like those were expensive. He knew because his ex had emphasized the blond streaks in her hair that way. And nothing about Jolene or her tastes had been cheap.

"By the way," Granny said, "someone made me an offer on the Nevada property."

Jared wasn't aware that she'd had any out-of-state land or holdings. "What property is that?"

"It's a large parcel that Everett purchased years ago." Everett was her late husband, a man who'd passed away just before Jared had been adopted, which meant Granny had owned the land for at least twenty years. "Didn't I tell you boys about it?"

Jared looked at Matt, who shook his head.

"Well, I plumb near forgot all about it. Everett bought it ages ago, although I can't remember exactly when."

"And someone wants to buy it?" Jared asked.

"Yep. And he's courtin' me, too."

Courting her? Jared furrowed his brow. "What do you mean?"

Granny laughed. "Not courting me like a moonstruck lover. He's just calling and sweet-talking me some, hoping I'll sell. And to tell you the truth, I think it's time. Everett said it would be a good investment for our old age."

"Where is it located?" Jared asked.

"Not too far from Las Vegas. Everett always thought the town would grow and that the property would be valuable someday."

"So do you want to sell?" he asked.

"If they make me a decent offer."

Jared feared, at her age, she might not be able to negotiate a real-estate deal—not without being taken advantage of. And who was to say what a "decent offer" was? "Why don't you let me talk to that guy the next time he calls?"

"All right." Granny took a sip of coffee, then watched as Connie took a platter of pancakes from the oven, where they'd been kept warm, and placed them on the table. Each one was an uneven shade of brown and shaped like the ink blots on a Rorschach test. Jared wondered if the hands had chosen the ones that looked more edible and left these behind.

"Hotcakes anyone?" Connie asked.

Matt merely stared at the stack, and Jared wondered if he'd make it until lunch if he didn't eat any of them.

"Thanks," Granny said, snagging one that was a little too dark around the edges for Jared's taste. "They're looking better each time you make them, Connie. I told you perfect flapjacks just take practice."

It seemed pretty apparent that Granny hadn't required her new cook to provide references.

Before long, they were joined at the table by Sabrina and her nephew, whose eyes widened when he spotted Jared. "We never get to eat with the cowboys." Then his gaze lit on Matt and his wheelchair.

Jared had to give the kid credit for biting his lip, rather than commenting.

After Granny made the introductions, Sabrina dug through the pile of hotcakes and found one shaped like an egg. It was a perfect shade of brown on one side, and nearly white on the other.

She placed it on the boy's plate, but he seemed more interested in Matt's chair. Curiosity grew in his eyes.

"My grandfather has a wheelchair," the boy finally said. "But it isn't as cool as yours."

"Mine's *pretty* cool," Matt said.

Was Jared the only one who sensed sarcasm in his brother's tone?

"What happened to you?" the boy asked. "My grandpa fell down and broke his hip."

"Matt broke his legs," Granny explained, probably assuming her middle son would shine the kid like he usually did when someone brought up the subject. Or maybe she was just trying to take the heat off him. "Thank God he won't have to stay in the chair forever."

Maybe not, although that was left to be seen. But either way, Matt would never compete in the rodeo again, which was his life. So Jared suspected his brother didn't get a whole lot of comfort from that. If he did, you'd think he'd be trying harder to get better.

"Have you started physical therapy again?" Granny asked.

Wrong question, Jared could have told her. But he didn't.

Matt tensed, then glanced at her, his expression blank. "No. Not yet."

Footsteps sounded, and the redhead—Tori—joined them at the table, taking a seat next to the boy.

"How'd you sleep last night?" Tori asked Granny.

"Only woke up once to use the bathroom," Granny said. "You were right about that medication."

"Good. I'm glad to hear it."

It was bad enough that three strangers had infiltrated Granny's life and home, but it was even worse to have them butting into her personal habits.

"Hey, cool," Joey said, as he pulled his fork out of the gooey middle of his hotcake. "They're cream-filled."

"Uh-oh. Sorry about that." The blond cook snatched away the boy's plate. "That's not cream filling, it's batter. I guess that one needs to be cooked a little more."

This was crazy. Jared wondered if Sabrina, the bookkeeper, knew how to run an adding machine or if Tori, the maid, knew which end of the broom was up.

He had to talk Granny into selling the ranch and moving in with him, where he could take care of her. Too bad she was every bit as stubborn as she was good-hearted.

A knock sounded at the door. Before waiting to be invited in, the ranch foreman entered the mudroom. "Sorry to interrupt breakfast, but Earl Clancy just split his head wide-open. He's refusing to go into town and see a doctor, but it looks pretty bad to me."

"He needs to go anyway," Sabrina said. "If he's worried about the cost, worker's compensation will take care of it."

Tori scooted her chair away from the table. "I'll go take a look at the wound. Maybe I can talk Earl into getting it checked."

"Thanks, ma'am." Lester turned toward the door and placed his hat back on his head. "I'd sure appreciate that."

The redhead reached into a cupboard near the refrigerator and pulled out a white metal box with a red cross on the front. Jared wondered if she had first-aid training, suspecting that she might have. Still, that didn't make her Florence Nightingale.

"You know," he said, getting to his feet, "I think I'll go check on the injured man myself. If he needs a doctor, I'll drive him into town."

And even if he didn't, Jared wanted to get the foreman off by himself. Lester Bailey had been working for the Rocking C for almost as long as Jared could remember, and if anyone had a handle on Granny's mental state, it was him.

"I'll keep the hotcakes warm for you," the cook said.

"Thanks, Connie. But don't bother." Jared would much rather pick up something to eat in town. As he reached the back door of the mudroom and grabbed his hat, footsteps sounded behind him.

"Wait a minute."

He turned to see Sabrina heading after him, a plastic container in her arms. "Why don't you take a couple of cookies with you? Think of them as a hearty bowl of oatmeal-on-the-run, only better."

Jared, who'd always had a sweet tooth, reached inside and pulled out one of the plumpest cookies he'd ever seen. "Who made these?"

"Connie did."

The cook?

"She's a whiz at making sweets and desserts. So I don't think one will be enough." She handed him a couple more.

He took the cookies she offered, then watched as she reached into the jar and pulled out one for herself. After taking a bite, she closed her eyes, relishing each chew.

Jared had never known that eating could be so damn sexy. His mind wandered to the vision Sabrina had made last night, wearing that flowing white nightgown and with that veil of hair sluicing over her shoulders and down her back.

Now, as she murmured a "Mmm" in delight, it set off a wave of hunger inside of him. And he wasn't talking about food.

But under the circumstances, the cookies would be a healthier choice.

## Chapter Three

Jared's talk with the foreman would have to wait until after he'd driven Earl Clancy, the injured ranch hand, into the Brighton Valley Urgent Care Center for stitches.

Not only did Tori seem to have a good handle on first aid, she also had a way of dealing with a tough-as-rawhide ranch hand who didn't want "folks fussin'" over him.

When cajoling the crotchety wrangler into seeking medical help hadn't worked, she got tough and slapped her hands on her hips. "Earl, don't be stubborn. That wound is going to get infected if you don't get it treated."

Lester eased closer. "Ma'am, I'm afraid they don't come any more hardheaded than Earl. About five years back, he lost his big toe when he didn't take care of an ingrown nail."

"Is that right?" Tori shifted her weight from one foot to the other. "Well, listen here, Earl. There's not a whole lot above the shoulders you're going to want them to amputate. Now, get into Mr. Clayton's truck and let him drive you to town."

Earl grumbled some, but he did as the woman ordered.

"You'll be back and mending that fence before you know it," Lester told him.

But in reality, Jared and Earl hadn't returned until just after lunch. Tori had called it right, though. She'd guessed it would take close to fifteen stitches to close the wound, and Jared had counted sixteen.

As they approached the barn, the truck hit a pothole in the driveway, and Earl rattled off an "Ow," followed by a few choice swear words. "I told that damn nurse I didn't need a tetanus shot, but she was as pushy as that redheaded maid. And just to be ornery, I think she hit a nerve in my rump. And now my backside hurts worse than my head."

Jared parked the truck near the barn, where one of the hands had left Earl's horse waiting for him, saddled and ready to go.

"You need any help?" he asked the man.

"Heck, no. I've had about all the tender lovin' care I need for the rest of my life."

Jared watched as Earl climbed onto his mount, wincing as he settled his butt in the saddle. As he rode off, Jared headed for the barn, looking for the foreman. He found him in his office, placing an order for feed and grain.

When Lester hung up the phone, Jared asked, "Got a minute?"

"Sure." Lester pointed at a green vinyl chair that sat across the desk from him. "Have a seat."

Jared thought about shutting the door, but decided it was just the two of them. When he sat down, he tossed out the question that had been bothering him since the night before. "How do you think Granny is doing? I'm talking both physically and mentally."

"All right, I suppose. But she's getting older, and bodies naturally wear out. I guess you could say she's slipping a bit."

"In what way?"

Lester glanced at the open doorway, then back at Jared. "She's been a little forgetful."

"Give me an example."

Lester lifted his battered Stetson, raked a hand through his thick, curly gray hair, then adjusted the hat back on his head. "Can't say as I remember anything in particular."

Maybe Doc had been mistaken.

"Then how do you know she's 'slipping'?" Jared asked.

"I just do. And it wouldn't hurt none if you and your brothers started coming around to visit more often."

"It might be best if I took her home to live with me."

Lester's eyes grew wide, and he slowly shook his head. "Nope. That won't work."

"Why not?"

"It just won't. That's all."

A lot of help he was. If Lester hadn't always been a man of few words, Jared might have thought the aging ranch foreman was slipping, too. "Thanks. I'll let you get back to work."

A glimmer of relief seemed to cross Lester's face, and

Jared left him to it. Maybe it was time to go into the house and have a little chat with both the maid and the cook.

As Jared left the barn and headed toward the porch, he spotted Sabrina's nephew playing with Sassy, one of two Australian shepherds that lived on the ranch.

With his mind on Granny and her well-being, Jared had no intention of stopping to talk, but the boy stood when he approached.

"Hey, mister. Can I ask you something?"

Jared's steps slowed. "What's that?"

"Are you a *real* cowboy?"

Jared had half a notion to tell him no and go about his business. There was no need to befriend a kid who wouldn't be living on the ranch that much longer—especially if Granny sold out and moved in with Jared.

But he remembered his own first days on the Rocking C, his own wide-eyed interest in horses and cowboys and ranch life. In fact, the day Clem Bixby had taken him under wing had turned Jared's life around and set the course of his future.

"I suppose you could call me a cowboy," he admitted to the kid.

"And you used to live here, right?"

"Yep."

"But you don't anymore?"

"I own my own spread about a hundred miles north of here." Jared wondered where the little guy was going with all the questions.

"Then I guess I'm allowed to talk to you all I want."

"What do you mean?" Jared asked.

"Sabrina said I can't bother the cowboys who live here because they're working."

So Jared was free game, huh?

The boy eased closer, his small hand lifted to shield the sun's glare from his eyes. "Can I ask you something else?"

Again, Jared thought about making an excuse and leaving, but what would it hurt to stick around for a minute or so longer? "Sure. Go ahead."

"Did you have to go to school to be a cowboy?"

A grin tugged at Jared's lips. "Not the kind of school with desks and teachers and homework, if that's what you mean. But I had a whole lot to learn, and it wasn't easy."

"Sabrina says I gotta go to college, but I didn't even like first grade. And I don't think second grade will be all that much fun, either."

"Oh, yeah?" Jared hadn't liked school, either. Not when he'd lived in Houston. It was a lot better when he attended Brighton Valley Elementary, he supposed, but he'd dreaded every minute he'd had to spend away from the ranch.

The boy clucked his tongue. "I'd rather stay here and watch the cowboys work all day long. Maybe, if I did that, they'd let me help round up cows and ride horses."

"Cowboys don't need a college degree," Jared said, "although it might help some. But second grade is important. You sure don't want to miss out on any of the basic lessons all cowboys ought to know."

"Like what?"

"Well," Jared said, rubbing his chin and trying to recall some of the things Clem had told him. "Let's say there's an auction and you're in need of a few good horses. They advertise those in the newspaper. If you couldn't read, you'd miss out."

"Maybe one of my cowboy friends could call me on the phone and tell me about it," the boy countered.

Sharp kid. Jared tried not to grin. "Okay, let's say they did. How are you going to know how much money you can afford to bid? You need to be able to add and subtract pretty well to balance your bank account."

"I could hire someone like Sabrina. She's really good at math and could do that stuff for me."

"But then you'd have to trust someone else with your money. What if they ran off with everything you owned?"

"Sabrina wouldn't."

Jared hoped the kid was right.

But in Jared's case, he'd learned that some women, like Jolene, couldn't be trusted. And when they ran off, they took more than a man's money.

They took his heart and his pride.


Jared fixed himself a glass of iced tea, then took a seat at the kitchen table and watched Connie dry the last of the lunch dishes.

"Have you seen my mother?" he asked the so-called cook.

"She took her mare out for an afternoon ride." Connie turned away from a three-layer cake she was frosting—a chocolate masterpiece that rivaled any of those in a bakery display case and put this morning's hotcakes to shame.

So what was the deal? She could make moist, chewy cookies and cakes, but couldn't whip up a decent meal for breakfast?

Jared cleared his throat. "Well, then, I guess I'll have to wait to talk to her until she gets back."

Connie nodded, then returned to her work.

Jared carried his glass into the living room, where Tori the housekeeper was dusting the shelves in the handcrafted bookcase that Granny's husband had built many years ago. Matt had parked his wheelchair near the big bay window that looked over the driveway. He was holding a *Western Horseman* magazine in his lap and gazing through the glass into the yard, yet by his expression, Jared suspected his thoughts were anywhere but in the here and now.

He did look up as Jared entered the room, though.

"Did you get that guy stitched up?" he asked.

"Yep. He's back on the job." Jared slid his thumbs into the front pocket of his jeans. "Have you had a chance to talk to Granny this morning?"

"Not really." Matt glanced to the bookshelf, where Tori stood on a footstool, her back to them. "She was busy outside for a while. Then, just after lunch, she saddled Bluebonnet and took off."

If Granny hadn't given up her daily afternoon ride, then maybe she was doing okay after all.

"She should be back in an hour or so," the redhead said, obviously listening.

Jared would have to choose his words carefully, although now might be a good time to quiz the maid and get a feel for the kind of person she was. So he made his way to the bookshelf. "Tori, you mentioned something about Granny's medication earlier, and I'm curious. What was that all about?"

The attractive redhead, stopped her work and turned, a dust rag dangling from her hands. "Granny was complaining about having to wake up at all hours of the night to use the bathroom, so I asked her what meds she was taking. When she showed me the prescription bottles, I suggested she take the diuretic in the morning. She noticed a big difference."

"What's a diuretic?" he asked, wondering if Doc was the one who was slipping.

"Some people refer to it as a water pill. It helps rid the body of excess fluids and sodium, or rather, salt. She's taking it along with a beta-blocker for hypertension."

Tori seemed to have a better than average handle on Granny's medication. And after seeing how she'd dealt with Earl, Jared suspected she'd definitely taken some kind of first-aid course. But now he was beginning to think she might have had more training than that. And if that were the case, then what was she doing working as a maid and not at a hospital or clinic?

"You seem to know a lot about medicine," he said. "Where'd you pick up all that knowledge?"

She paused for a moment, then shrugged. "I read a lot."

As she returned to her work, providing him a view of her back, he pondered her response. She'd evaded his question, which made him wonder why she was holding back—and what other secrets she might have.

Tori was a pretty gal, with big blue eyes, a scatter of freckles across her nose and long, curly red hair pulled back with a clip.

Jared slid a glance Matt's way, only to find that his brother was watching Tori, as well. A hint of masculine interest in Matt's eyes suggested he found her attractive, and that he had noticed the way her snug denim jeans did justice to a pair of long legs and a sexy rear.

That was a good sign, Jared decided. Tori was the

first woman his brother had seemed to notice since the accident. Not that Jared would encourage anything. His brother wasn't ready for any kind of relationship, although it was a relief to know he might seek happiness with someone new in the future.

Of course, whether he found it or not was another question.

As for Jared, himself, Jolene had done a real number on him, so he doubted if he'd ever trust another woman again.

And although Jared suspected Tori hadn't been entirely honest with him about her medical background, when it came to stealing from Granny, that didn't make her any more of a suspect than Sabrina.

Any of the employees, particularly those with free rein in the household, could have taken Granny's money, yet the pretty, dark-haired bookkeeper was still the most logical.

Jared was open-minded, though. And if Sabrina hadn't stolen the money, she was also the most likely to help him find the real culprit.

Leaving his brother and Tori in the living room, he headed back down the hall to the office, where Sabrina worked at the computer.

The prim brunette was so intent on what she was doing that she apparently hadn't heard him walk up. So he watched her for a while, intrigued by the way she ran the tip of her tongue across her full bottom lip.

He decided not to interrupt her just yet, not while he was enjoying the view, but she glanced up and caught him looking at her.

"Got a minute?" he asked.

"Sure. Come on in."

He took a seat across from her and decided to lay the problem on the line and gauge her reaction. "I heard that Grant Whitaker found some discrepancies in Granny's account. There's some money missing."

"I'm aware of that." Sabrina straightened and leaned back in the desk chair. "Mr. Whitaker mentioned it to me a couple of days ago, but when I asked your mother about having an ATM card or utilizing the online banking service, she didn't have any idea what I was talking about."

"Then someone unauthorized must have ATM access to her account."

"You might be right, but your mother has been pretty forgetful lately. Just yesterday, I learned of an account she didn't even remember opening."

"How did you find out about it?"

"She received a letter from a savings and loan located in another town, telling her that the account would be frozen due to nonactivity."

Jared leaned against the doorjamb and crossed his arms. "I thought you went through her files. Wasn't there any record of statements being sent to her?"

"I might have missed it, but I don't think so." Sabrina pushed her chair from the desk and stood. In the course of her workday, a button on her blouse had become undone, and Jared couldn't help noticing a flash of skin and the white lace trim of her bra.

"I asked the bank to trace those withdrawals," she said. "I was told they were all made from an ATM card that your mother requested, a card someone activated through the main branch."

The question was, who had done that?

Sabrina was supposedly checking in to it, but Jared thought it might be a better idea if he stopped by the main branch himself. One of the girls he'd gone to school with used to be married to the vice president of the bank. Hopefully, she still was, although he knew the stats on break ups these days better than anyone.

The phone rang, and Sabrina reached across the desk to grab the receiver.

"Good afternoon. Rocking C Ranch." She paused, her body still bent, her blouse gaping open even more than before and revealing the gentle swell of a breast. A man would thank his lucky stars to cup his hand around the soft fullness of her flesh, to stroke, caress…

Damn. He tore his gaze away before she realized he'd been lusting over her.

"No," Sabrina told the caller, "she's not in right now. But if you leave your name and number, I'll pass along the message." She reached for a pink pad and pen. "Sure. I'll let Mrs. Clayton know you called."

As she hung up the phone and straightened, she turned toward him, the pink sheet of paper in her hand. As she did so, the pen she'd been using rolled off the desk.

"Oops." She stooped to pick it up from the floor, giving Jared a view of her from the rear.

His eyes fixed on the way the fabric of her slacks stretched across shapely hips.

Not bad, he thought. Not bad at all.

But Sabrina wasn't someone he ought to be looking at—from the front or the rear. At least not until she'd earned his trust, which could take years.

And he expected to have the problems solved at the Rocking C within a week, if not sooner.

* * *

After Sabrina had shut down the computer for the day and left the office, she went to look for Joey so they could spend some time together before dinner.

He tended to gravitate to the outdoors, so she usually knew right where to find him. Her rules were firm, though. He must always stay in the front yard and be able to see the porch.

It hadn't taken her long to spot him. He was sitting in the shade of an elm tree that grew in the middle of the lawn, one of the ranch dogs resting beside him.

"Are you up for an adventure?" she asked. "Mrs. Clayton mentioned that one of the broodmares is going to foal soon, and I thought it might be fun to take a look at her."

"Sure." Joey brightened. "Can Sassy go with us?"

"Sassy?"

"My dog."

Sabrina bent to scratch the Australian shepherd's ear. "Sassy belongs to Mrs. Clayton, Joey. And when we leave the ranch, she'll stay here."

"I know." Regret laced his voice. "But I can pretend, can't I?"

Just as long as he remembered they weren't permanent residents at the Rocking C. Sabrina might be trying her best to fit in and be accepted, to find a small piece of the ranch that they could call home, but eventually she wanted a place that belonged only to her. A place from which no one could ever make her leave.

"When we move into a house of our own, you can have a pet."

"Okay. I'd like a dog and a horse. Maybe a cat, too."

"A lot will depend upon where we move. Horses need a much bigger yard than most animals."

As they neared the white wooden fence that corralled the broodmares, a rider on horseback approached.

But not just any rider. It was Jared.

Seated atop a chestnut gelding, the sun at his back, he was a commanding sight. A woman, Sabrina realized, didn't have to be attracted to the rugged, outdoorsy type to perk up when she noticed him.

He tipped his hat in John Wayne fashion.

"Hi, Mr. Clayton." Joey started toward the man with a spring in his step. "Did you take your horse out for a run?"

A hint of a smile softened the rancher's face as he studied the wide-eyed child. "It wasn't a pleasure ride this time. I went to check on Earl, who's still out mending fences."

"How's he doing?" Sabrina asked. "He should be taking it easy after that accident."

"That crusty old wrangler is still hopping mad about wasting half a day at the clinic and about not being able to give one hundred percent because an uppity nurse insisted upon crippling him with a hypodermic needle in the…" He glanced at Joey, then cleared his throat. "Well, I guess you don't need a direct quote."

"I get the idea." Sabrina couldn't help but grin. "Thanks for taking him. If you wouldn't have done it, I might have had to drive him to see a doctor. And I have a feeling it wouldn't have been a fun trip."

"Earl's a tough old bird." Jared lifted his hat and raked a hand through his hair. "By the way, did you hear anything back from the bank?"

"No. Not yet. But I talked to Granny earlier and quizzed her about the accounts she has. She thinks there are about four or five, but isn't sure." The elderly woman had also given Sabrina permission to discuss any of her financial business with her son, which was the only reason why this conversation was taking place.

Jared's horse stepped to the right, no longer blocking the sun.

Sabrina lifted a hand to her eyes, trying to lessen the glare. "By the way, when I went back through last year's expenses, I saw property tax payments for that Las Vegas parcel. So if she forgot about owning it, her memory lapse was recent."

Jared replaced the hat on his head, then dismounted. "I was afraid of that. I asked her about having an ATM card, and she didn't seem to know what I was talking about."

"I'm inclined to believe her. But then again, if her memory is failing…" Sabrina looked at Jared. "Well… You know what I mean."

Unfortunately, Jared knew exactly what she meant. But he didn't want to believe it. Or accept it.

On the outside, it appeared that he and Sabrina had broached some kind of alliance, when in fact, he merely wanted to win her confidence.

He still wasn't convinced that she wasn't the one stealing from Granny. Hopefully, she wasn't. But he still didn't trust her. Not yet.

Maybe not ever.

As he prepared to cool down the gelding, he looked at the boy, who was gazing at him and the horse with stars in his eyes.

Joey was rail-thin, and a bit fairer than his pretty aunt, whose Latina roots were evident in a flawless, olive complexion. He also seemed a bit frail for ranch life, although he'd made no secret of his appreciation for horses and cowboys.

"If it's all right with your aunt," Jared told the child, "I'll give you a ride around the yard."

Joey's eyes widened, and he threw a pleading gaze at Sabrina. "Please, oh, please?"

"If Mr. Clayton doesn't mind…"

"I don't." Jared was going to suggest that Joey call him by his first name, but there was no need in them getting that familiar. Not when the length of Sabrina's employment was still in question.

He had no intention of going to the trouble of teaching the boy how to mount. Instead, he lifted him onto the saddle.

Joey gripped the saddle horn with both hands, his bright-eyed, ear-to-ear grin a dead giveaway that he was in hog heaven. "This is the very first time I ever rode a horse."

If anyone could understand his excitement, it was Jared.

As he began to lead the gelding around the yard, giving the kid a ride, he stole a glance at Sabrina. She smiled and mouthed a "Thank you."

He gave her a little shrug. It was no big deal.

"Do they give lessons on how to ride horses?" Joey asked.

"Yes, there are ranches and stables that teach people how to ride."

"Does it cost a lot of money?"

"It varies."

"Is it hard to learn?"

"Not for a cowboy." Jared glanced up at the kid. "And you seem to be a natural."

That wasn't quite true, but what would it hurt to make the kid's smile last a little longer?

"I'd like lessons, but Aunt Sabrina won't let me ask anyone here at the ranch to teach me. She doesn't want us to wear out our welcome. I mean, we're welcome to be here and all, but you know."

"You mean, she doesn't want you to take advantage of Mrs. Clayton's good nature?"

"Yeah. I guess. We're living here now, and Mrs. Clayton told me I could call her Granny and everything. So it's kind of like we're friends, you know? But Sabrina is big on manners and stuff."

"Oh, yeah?"

"Yeah. I think she even read a book on it and everything."

Jared couldn't prevent an almost-silent chuckle from erupting in his chest. Kids, he supposed, had an interesting view of life.

He led the horse around the side of the barn, then along the corral until he reached the outbuildings. When he figured they'd been walking for a good five minutes, he thought it wouldn't hurt to end the ride. But something wouldn't let him.

"You see that black mare in the corral?" he asked.

"Uh-huh. She's really pretty, but her stomach looks a little bit fat."

Jared chuckled. "That's because she's going to foal."

"You mean, she has a baby inside her?" The boy

turned his head to take a good look at the broodmare and shifted in the saddle.

Jared quickly grabbed a hold of Joey's foot to steady him. "Careful, sport."

"Oops."

"Hang on, will you? Your aunt would skin me alive if I let you fall off."

"She wouldn't be happy about it. But you could probably take her if she got *really* mad."

He could take her, all right. The thought of things getting physical between the two of them was an intriguing vision, though. And fighting wasn't what he had in mind. "You're right, Joey. I'm a lot bigger and stronger than she is, but real cowboys know how to treat a lady."

"You know what, Mr. Clayton?"

"What's that?"

"I never knew a real live cowboy before. And I'll bet you're the best in the whole wide world."

Jared hadn't been the subject of hero worship in some time—not since Greg was a boy—and it...well, it kind of touched him.

Maybe that's why he spent the next half hour wandering all over the ranch on foot, leading the kid around like an old man giving pony rides at the fair.

But what the hell.

When Jared finally wound up back at the barn, where Sabrina waited, she cast him a pretty smile that darn near turned him inside out. It was as if she saw him as some kind of hero, too.

And for some crazy reason, that touched him even more.

## Chapter Four

Jared stretched out on the sofa in the den, the only room in the house that wasn't taken, and read a leatherbound volume of *Moby Dick*. He hadn't been able to sleep and didn't feel like watching television.

Outside, footsteps sounded on the front porch. He glanced at the clock on the lamp table, noting it was nearly midnight. So he set the novel aside and got up to peer out the window. Obviously, the dogs had decided that whoever was prowling around could be trusted to move about after dark.

When he drew back the curtains, he spotted Sabrina. She was facing the railing and looking out into the yard. Unlike last night, she wore a robe to cover her nightgown. But her ebony hair hung as long and loose as before.

The light of a full moon gave her a mystical aura, and a lovely one at that.

He watched from behind the glass for a while, then turned from the window and made his way down the hall and into the living room, where a lamp glowed softly. On the coffee table, an empty glass with traces of milk sat next to small plate bearing chocolate crumbs. Sabrina, he concluded, had been snacking.

The house was quiet save for the ticktock of the antique clock over the mantel. So, out of respect for those who were fast asleep, he carefully swung open the screen door. But the hinges screeched unexpectedly, causing Sabrina to gasp and nearly jump out of her shoes—if she'd been wearing them.

"Oh. Jared." The breathy, almost sensual, sound of his name as it slid from her lips stirred something deep inside of him. Something that had been dormant long before Jolene had walked out on him and moved back to Vegas.

Sabrina placed a hand over her heart. "You scared me half to death."

"Sorry. I didn't mean to." He eased toward her. "What are you doing out here?"

"Nothing." She gave a little shrug. "Sometimes I have trouble sleeping."

Like she had last night? "Why's that?"

"I don't know. Too much on my mind, I suppose. It's something I've had to deal with most of my life."

He closed the gap between them and joined her at the railing. Her scent, something shower-fresh and floral, laced the night air and set his senses reeling. He started to comment on her choice of lotion or soap, to tell her that he liked it, then clamped his mouth shut.

There was no need to make her think he was interested in her as a woman, even if his hormones insisted that, at this very moment, he was.

"I suppose Joey has already gone to bed," he said, trying to ditch any evidence of sexual attraction.

"Unlike me, that little boy can sleep anywhere."

"What's the matter? Isn't your mattress comfortable?" He figured that might be the case. He didn't like sleeping on the sofa in the den, but the only other option had been the barn, and that would be a whole lot worse.

"The bed isn't a problem. You'd think after all the different places I've lived in the past that I'd be able to sleep standing up." A little chuckle slipped out, but he guessed it was more from nervousness than actual humor.

"I take it you moved around a lot when you were younger."

"Yes, quite a bit. But it didn't seem to affect Carlos, my twin brother. He became a long-haul trucker."

"Is Carlos the boy's father?"

"Yes." She shifted her body, not exactly facing him, but no longer standing at his side. "Suzy, his mom, passed away nearly six months ago."

"From what?"

Sabrina cocked her head to the side and slid him an assessing glance, as though he was being a little too curious. But he couldn't help it. There was a lot he wanted to know.

"Suzy had a heart attack. It was sudden and completely unexpected. Joey never had a chance to say goodbye."

Jared blew out a little whistle. "Wow. How old was she?"

"Only twenty-two." Sabrina turned, resting her back against the railing. "The doctor said that she'd had a heart defect for years. And apparently, it had never been diagnosed."

"It must have been tough on Joey."

"It was."

"What about his father?"

"Carlos took some time off to attend the funeral, but it wasn't as long as he would have liked. He had to go back to work."

Leaving his son in the care of his twin sister. "If the boy needs him, maybe he ought to find another line of work. One that's closer to home."

Sabrina tensed. "It's tough supporting a family and providing health insurance when you don't have a high-school diploma."

Why was that? Sabrina obviously saw the value of an education. And her twin was a dropout?

"I'm sure it is. But it seems to me that a boy needs a dad, too."

"Believe me, Carlos would be here with Joey if he could."

Jared nearly asked why he couldn't, but let it go. Something told him that she wouldn't appreciate being prodded with more questions, no matter how many he had.

"Thanks for giving Joey that ride today," she said, changing the subject. "You have no idea how badly he wants a horse of his own."

Probably as badly as Jared had wanted one when he first came to the Rocking C. "No problem. He's a good kid."

She grew still for a moment, her gaze lifting to his and setting his senses on edge.

The night wind, as light as it was, blew a strand of hair across her cheek, and she brushed it aside. "Carlos loves his son more than anything. I want you to understand that."

Jared nodded, as though he did understand. But his childhood experience didn't allow him to be sympathetic for Joey's father, no matter how far Sabrina went to defend him.

When Jared's biological mother died, he'd been sent to Houston to live with his father, a man who'd gotten involved with drug dealers and had put his kid in foster care "for a little while."

"Just long enough for me to make a new start," he'd told Jared when he'd left him at a county office. But he'd never come back.

So rather than offer an opinion, Jared clamped his mouth shut. Families ought to stick together.

No matter what.

The wind kicked up a bit, sending another wisp of Sabrina's hair across her cheek, but rather than wait for her to sweep it away, he risked doing so himself. His fingers trailed across the softness of her skin.

Her breath caught, and their gazes locked. Her lips parted, as though she was going to say something, but no words came out.

His pulse began to pound out a ragged, primal beat, and his blood rushed through his veins, warming steadily.

The moment was too still, too tempting.

All he had to do was tilt her chin up, sweep his lips across hers. And he damn near had a mind to do it.

So why didn't she step back? Draw away?

It sure would have been easier if she would have told him where he could get off. Or if she would have made an excuse to head back into the house.

As it was, he had to do something himself. Something that didn't seem natural.

He let his hand drop to his side, empty. "Well, I guess I'd better turn in. I've got an early day tomorrow."

"Sleep tight," she said.

Yeah, right. He doubted he'd get any rest at all, because as much as he wanted to pat himself on the back for winning a daring battle with temptation, he had a feeling he'd be kicking himself all the way back to the den.


Sabrina remained on the porch for another few minutes before heading back into the house. All the while, she relived those last couple of moments with Jared on the porch.

He'd nearly kissed her; she'd been sure of it.

Not that she had all that much experience with men and romance. After the mistakes her parents had made, something for which she and Carlos were still paying a price, she knew better than to risk getting seriously involved with anyone until after she graduated and had a solid grip on her life and her future.

In the past, it hadn't been difficult to shy away from men and relationships. She'd just kept her nose in the books and her mind on her goal. But she'd never been faced with a rugged cowboy, whose musky, leathery scent set off something warm and fluttery in her chest, and she was afraid that keeping her focus might not be as easy on the ranch as it had been at the University of Houston.

Now, more than ever, a romance would be an unnecessary complication in her life. Especially when she found herself interested in a man who had a bossy, stubborn streak that brought out the worst in her. A man who threatened what little stability she'd found on the Rocking C.

Of course, he had a tender side, too.

"He's loyal to a fault," Mrs. Clayton had said about her oldest son, and Sabrina had reason to believe that might be true. His kindness had certainly been evident today as she'd watched him lead Joey and the horse around the ranch.

It was nice to see a grown man interact with a child like that, something Sabrina and her brother had missed out on while growing up.

But at this point in her life, she wasn't ready to open her heart to any obscure romantic possibilities. She wanted—and *needed*—to establish a home and a career first.

Still, in spite of her reluctance to allow herself to get involved with anyone, there'd been something almost magical about standing outside under the spell of a lover's moon. And Sabrina realized that if Jared had indeed tried to kiss her while they'd been on the porch, she just might have let him.

And then where would she be?

She looked over her shoulder to the far right, where a light burned beyond the curtain that draped the window in the den. Jared had said he was going to turn in for the night, but she suspected he hadn't done so yet.

Still, she didn't want to stay on the porch, where his presence seemed to remain long after he'd gone. She had a feeling that if she closed her eyes, she just might catch a lingering whiff of his scent. And that if she reached out, she might be able to touch him. To slide her hand around the back of his neck and draw his lips to hers.

So for that reason, she decided to return to the house and lock the door behind her. Stopping near the lamp table, she picked up the glass and plate she'd used earlier and carried them back to the kitchen, where she washed them and put them away.

As she tiptoed down the hall to her room, her steps slowed near the closed door of the den. As much as she'd like to write off Jared Clayton, to ignore the sexual curiosity he stirred in her, she couldn't.

She wondered when he and his brother would leave. It would certainly make her life easier when they did. But even then, she would still be living in someone else's house, eating someone else's food, following someone else's rules.

*Shh!* she remembered her mother telling her and Carlos as kids. *You're making too much noise,* niños. *Tío Jose will get tired of it and make us move.*

*Stay out of Abuelito's flower garden,* they'd been instructed time and again.

*Don't touch those knickknacks. Your* prima *Luisa is afraid you'll get them dirty or break them.*

Children adjust to rules, she supposed, but the instructions she and her brother had received changed from one house to another. So she and Carlos soon learned not to wear out their welcomes because, when they did, it was time to move all over again—to a new home, a new neighborhood, a new school.

As Sabrina quietly let herself into the bedroom she

and Joey had been assigned, she studied the gentle rise and fall of the little boy's chest as he slept, unaware of the past, oblivious to the cold ache of discomfort Sabrina felt in someone else's home.

She brushed a kiss across his brow, then turned away, removed her robe and climbed into the bed that had been provided for her.

Just last week, Mrs. Clayton had mentioned the empty cabin again.

"No one has lived there since Clem passed on, which has been a good ten years," she'd said. "so as soon as I get around to cleaning it, you and Joey can move in."

Sabrina hadn't wanted to rush her, but maybe it was time to do so now. She would offer to spend the weekend scrubbing the cabin herself. Hopefully, Mrs. Clayton would see the wisdom in the plan.

Besides the privacy she craved, there was another logical reason she should move out of the ranch house.

No good could come of her and Jared bumping into each other at all hours of the day and night. She lifted her fingers to her lips, tried to imagine the press of his mouth against hers.

She was afraid it was just a matter of time before they met again when the rest of the household was asleep, when defenses were down and vulnerabilities lay open.

And who knew what temptations might lurk under the silvery light of another lover's moon?

The next morning, Jared joined the ranch hands for breakfast, where the conversation was mostly small talk about the weather and the likelihood of rain on Sunday. No one made any comment about the meal laid before them, other than "Pass the salt" or "Hand over more ketchup, will ya?"

Connie had scrambled eggs and fried ham today. As usual, the moment she'd put the meal on the table, she'd skedaddled. And Jared could certainly understand why.

The ham, while unevenly sliced, wasn't half-bad, but the eggs were rubbery, and the toast both looked and tasted like buttered shingles. So Jared figured he'd let the working men have their fill before he dug in and chose to start with coffee.

Before he finished his second cup, Matt wheeled himself into the room, just as the foreman and the hands took off to start their day.

Jared made room for the wheelchair at the table. "Good morning."

Matt nodded in greeting. At least he hadn't barked, "What's so good about it?" That was a response Jared had gotten a time or two.

"Did you sleep okay last night?" Jared asked, making chitchat. He hoped Matt's mood was lifting now that he was back at the Rocking C, but something told him it hadn't and that Jared was expecting too much.

"I slept all right," Matt said. "How about you?"

"Like a rock," Jared lied. When he'd finally quit thinking about the kiss he'd nearly stolen... Well, he couldn't say that Sabrina would have been caught unawares or that she would have been unwilling. By the look in her eyes, he figured she'd wanted that kiss as badly as he had.

And that was the problem.

It's not as if Jared had sworn off women after Jolene took off, but he sure wasn't going to get involved with another one right away. And certainly not one he didn't know very well.

He'd met Jolene during one of the yearly trips to Las Vegas he took with some of the men who owned ranches near his. He'd never been what you'd call a gambler, although he did enjoy playing blackjack and poker once in a while and was more lucky than not.

But that was at cards. If he'd learned anything at all from a hasty marriage and subsequent divorce, it had been not to gamble on women.

Jolene had been a showgirl, with great legs, long blond hair, a sexy smile and, according to her, a fondness for cowboys.

They'd met in a bar at Caesar's Palace after one of her performances and had hit it off. He supposed you could say they had chemistry. They'd shared a few laughs, and one visit to Las Vegas to see her had led to another.

Looking back, he now realized their heated affair had been destined to crash and burn eventually. But one night on a whim—okay, so they'd both been drunk and decided to give forever a try—they'd stopped by the Golden Heart Wedding Chapel and made it legal.

But Jolene had loved the Las Vegas nightlife and the glamour of the stage. And whatever had burned hot through the end of their short honeymoon had fizzled shortly after she'd moved to Texas and got a real taste of ranch life.

Nearly kissing Sabrina last night had triggered a slew of bad memories that had kept Jared staring at the ceiling until almost dawn. But ironically, switching back to thoughts of Sabrina and the flicker of desire he'd seen in her eyes had finally taken him to a place where he was able to drift off to dreamland.

Still, Jared had slept like crap and woke up with a crick in both his back and his neck. But no need to complain about something that would ease once he walked it off. His brother, on the other hand, wasn't going to be that lucky—that is, if Matt ever decided to give his legs another workout.

The doctor had suggested physical therapy, but after the first session, Matt had refused to go back or talk about his reasons for doing so. Jared doubted it was because of the pain or hard work. Matt was one of the toughest men he'd ever known.

In a way, he still was.

Jared got up and poured his brother a cup of coffee, then brought it back to the table, along with a clean plate.

Matt peered at the platter in the center of the table and scrunched his face. "What the hell is that?"

"Scrambled eggs, I think." Jared grabbed a serving spoon and scooped out a helping for his brother.

Matt blocked his efforts with a high-five hand. "That's plenty. Something tells me I'm only going to want enough to keep my stomach from grinding on itself."

Jared chuckled. It was nice to have something humorous to share with his brother these days. It had been a long time since either of them had found a reason to laugh.

Footsteps sounded, and Jared looked to the doorway, where Joey entered the room.

When their gazes met, the boy's face lit up like a blasted Fourth-of-July fireworks show. "Hey, Mr. Clayton. Is it okay if I sit down with you guys? Or should I wait until after you're finished?"

"No, go ahead. You like eggs?"

Joey shook his head. "Are there any of those cookies left?"

"Good thinking," Matt said. "Better yet, I wonder if there's any more of that chocolate cake we had at dinner last night. I don't feel much like eggs this morning, either."

As Jared hunted for the leftover dessert, Joey said, "I wish I was at school."

"Oh, yeah?" Jared found what he'd been looking for next to the bread box. "Why is that?"

"So I could tell all my friends that me and a real live cowboy had chocolate cake for breakfast."

Jared carried his find back to the table and used a knife to cut three pieces. "Well, you'd have to tell them that you ate with two of us. You might not know this, but my brother Matt is a bronc rider."

"No way," Joey said, turning his focus to the man in the wheelchair. "Really?"

"Yep." Jared served the cake. "And he's got a glass case full of silver belt buckles to prove it."

The boy, his brown eyes wide and glimmering, was speechless.

"That was a long time ago," Matt said.

"Oh," the boy said. "You mean, 'cause you got hurt? Did a bronc buck you off and step on your legs?"

"No."

Joey gave the answer some thought. "Then what happened?"

Jared held his tongue. He hadn't started this conversation for any reason other than to give Joey a bit of a thrill. But things had taken an unexpected turn. Still, he figured he'd been bailing out Matt long enough, and maybe it was time his brother faced the facts. Cindy and Tommy were gone. And Matt was never going to compete in another rodeo.

"How'd you get your legs hurt?" the boy asked, prodding for an answer.

"I was in a car accident." Matt's gaze turned dark, cold and quiet, as though he wanted the memories to stay buried with his fiancée and her son.

Footsteps sounded again, giving them all a reprieve, it seemed. As Jared searched the door for an excuse to find something else to talk about, he spotted Sabrina.

He couldn't help but study her, noticing she'd put on a pair of jeans and a pale-blue cotton shirt. Her hair had been woven into a long braid that hung down her back. She'd dressed casually today, and it made her look as though she belonged here—even if the jury was still out on that.

"Good morning," she said, as she headed for the coffeepot.

"Can you please get me a glass of milk?" Joey asked.

"Sure." She offered him a smile, then froze in her tracks. "Joey? What are you doing?"

The boy's grin bore a smear of chocolate frosting on his lips. "Eating breakfast with two of the best cowboys in the whole wide world."

"Did you have any eggs yet?"

"Nope," Joey said. "Me and the guys decided we'd rather have cake."

"I can't let you eat sweets for breakfast," she told the little wannabe cowboy.

"Why not?" Jared wasn't exactly sure why he felt

compelled to jump to the kid's defense. Some kind of Cowboy Code, he supposed. Or maybe because he'd been the one to cut and serve the cake.

"It's important to have a healthy, balanced meal to start the day," she said.

"But you ate cookies for breakfast yesterday," Jared reminded her. "And you even passed a few to me."

"That's because they were made out of oatmeal, which is clearly breakfast food." She crossed her arms, and tossed him a pretty frown.

Jared ought to let it drop, but he couldn't help stirring the pot. "I could be wrong, but chocolate cake has eggs in it. And I do believe this is buttercream frosting. All of which is clearly breakfast food, too."

She shifted her weight to one denim-clad hip. "Maybe I ought to let you chase him around if he gets hyper from all that sugar."

"I'll just lasso the little buckaroo and wait 'til he calms down." Jared couldn't help but grin. "Come on, Sabrina, ease up on the kid." He nodded toward the platter of eggs that were not only rubbery also but growing cold. "What do you think that grub is going to do to him?"

Before Sabrina could offer an argument, Granny entered the kitchen. "Well, now. Look at you, Sabrina. Finally wearing those clothes I bought you. You ought to be a whole lot more comfortable today."

"Actually," Sabrina said, "I was going to ask you if it would be all right if I went out to the cabin this morning and spent some time cleaning it up."

"Oh, I hate to have you do that," Granny said. "It's gonna be a real mess."

"I don't mind the work," Sabrina countered. "In fact, I'm looking forward to the exercise."

"Why are you volunteering?" Jared asked.

"Because Joey and I are going to move into it, but your mother doesn't want us to do that until it's clean. And I really don't mind." She brushed her hands along her hips.

"It's too much work for a woman," Granny said. "It's going to need some repairs, too."

"You might need some rattraps," Matt added. "No telling what moved in after Clem died."

Sabrina scrunched her face, obviously not nearly as eager to deal with a few critters than she was to scrub walls and mop floors.

"Jared," Granny said, "do you have any pressing plans this morning?"

Uh-oh. Granny was going to suggest that he help.

Of course, the sooner he got Sabrina out of the house the better. And if a few field mice—or whatever—made her reconsider living on the ranch and call it quits... Hey, that would solve half his problems right there.

Either way, if she moved out, freeing up the guest bedroom, he could get off the sofa in the den.

"Sure," he said, "I'd be glad to help."

"I hate to put you out," Sabrina replied.

"Actually, I wouldn't mind moving into your bedroom."

"I bet you wouldn't," Matt muttered.

"That's not what I meant."

But the idea, now that Matt brought it to mind, was far more appealing than Jared wanted it to be.

## Chapter Five

Armed with cleaning supplies, mops, brooms, rags and buckets, Sabrina and Jared made their way to the small, clapboard building that everyone on the ranch referred to as "the cabin."

The structure sat on a knoll in a pasture about a hundred yards from the house. Neglect and weather had done a real number on the exterior, but Sabrina didn't care. She could envision it with a fresh coat of white paint, a pot of geraniums on the stoop and new curtains on the windows.

The yard wasn't too bad. A splatter of wildflowers at the side of the house added color. And thanks to the grazing cattle, the weeds had been kept to a minimum.

As they drew closer, Jared's steps slowed and he studied the cabin as though it were an aged photograph that had been misplaced and recently found.

"It's been about ten years since I've been inside this place," he said, carefully scanning the building from its block foundation to its roof. "But I have a feeling it's going to take a lot more than a weekend to make it livable again."

Sabrina didn't mind the time or the work. She'd been dying to have some privacy all of her life. And while this house wasn't officially hers, it was the closest thing she'd ever had.

As she began to step onto the porch, Jared grabbed her arm and held her back, the intensity of his touch sending a shiver of heat through her veins.

"Be careful," he said. "That wood is rotten."

She glanced at the flooring, which was cracked and bowed by age and neglect. Most of the planks appeared as though they would give way with the least bit of weight.

"Then how do you suggest we get inside?" she asked.

He stooped and reached for one of the boards, pulling at it with his bare hands until he'd ripped it away. Then he tore off several more strips of wood. "How's that?" He straightened and brushed his palms together several times. "I'll go into town later this afternoon and bring back enough lumber to rebuild the porch. But I have a feeling that's not even half of what will need to be done if we really want to get this place back into shape."

Nevertheless, Sabrina was still glad to have a place of her own. "As long as it's clean, I can move in and deal with the repairs as one fix-it project at a time."

"Maybe we better see what we're up against." He

stepped into the gap made by the missing planks of wood and opened the door, which, apparently, no one had seen a reason to lock.

As Sabrina began to follow his steps, he turned and reached out to her. She thought he was being a gentleman, intent on steadying her steps. Instead he slid his hands around her waist.

Her breath caught as he lifted her off the ground and swung her around. Her hands inadvertently went to his shoulders to brace herself, where she felt the bulk of well-honed muscles flexing beneath a soft cotton shirt.

As he set her down inside the house, she faced him, cheeks warm, heart pounding, senses reeling. Finding her tongue was going to be a struggle.

A glint of humor lit his eyes, and a smile tweaked one corner of his lips. "I figured we didn't need to risk another worker's-compensation claim."

She doubted liability issues had anything to do with his actions, but wasn't going to challenge his motivation. Not when her heart was still ricocheting throughout her chest.

Hoping to take some control of her response to his presence and touch, she cleared her throat and turned to scan the inside of her new home, where a layer of dust covered the floors and sparse furnishings.

"Damn." Jared lifted his hat and raked a hand through his hair. "I don't even know where to begin."

"Let's start by getting some air in here. It's musty and stale."

After they each wrestled with a couple of windows that were covered with a hazy film of grime and hadn't been opened in ages, Sabrina assessed her surroundings. The living room was small, with a bare minimum of furniture—a black Naugahyde sofa, a green recliner and a floor lamp in the corner. A television set rested on a shelf made out of boards stacked on cinder blocks.

She strode to the bedroom, which boasted a chest of drawers and a queen-size bed with a blue corduroy spread. The first thing she'd need to do was change the linen and turn the mattress.

Next, she went into the bathroom, which had an olive green sink and matching toilet, as well as a white tub with rust marks near the drain. With a little elbow grease, she'd have the room spic-and-span, but the faucets appeared to be fused by lime deposits. Hopefully, Jared knew something about plumbing.

In the hall, she found a small linen closet full of towels and sheets—no longer fresh and clean but still folded. Once they were laundered and hung out on the line to dry, she would feel comfortable using them.

Continuing her inspection, she moved to the kitchen, which would also take some work. The pea-green Formica countertops were chipped in spots, but they would clean up nicely.

A peek in the cupboards revealed dishes, dusty from lack of use. Pots and pans, too. She looked in the built-in pantry and found canned goods that had swollen to the point of leaking. "Oh, yuck."

"Where do you want me to start?" Jared called out.

"Wherever you like." Sabrina returned to the living room, where Jared stood by the mantel. He was gazing at a Polaroid photograph he'd found.

"What's that?" she asked.

"A picture of Clem." His voice was husky yet soft. "And of me."

"Can I see it?"

He nodded and handed it to her. It showed an older man—a full-fledged cowboy, judging by his apparel—and Jared as a boy. They stood beside two horses.

Young Jared balanced a fishing pole in one hand, and held his catch with the other. The smile he wore reminded her of the one he'd sported in the picture his mother kept over the fireplace in her living room.

"You were a cute kid." She gave it back to him, and he placed it on the mantel, propping it up against the wall.

She couldn't help thinking that he'd grown up to be an even better-looking man, but she kept that thought to herself.

"Well," he said, "standing around won't get us anywhere."

He grabbed the broom and began to sweep the floor, sending flecks of dust dancing along a ray of sunlight that shined through the open window.

Sabrina headed for the kitchen, where she'd decided to scour the sink and countertops first. The dishes and utensils would all need to be washed, but she wanted a clean place to put them.

As she went to work, wetting a cloth, then dumping cleanser into both sides of the sink, she began making a mental list of all that needed to be done. It didn't take long to realize that she ought to be using paper and a pencil.

Yet she easily imagined herself moving in by tomorrow evening. Maybe she'd even pick a few wildflowers, put them into a glass of water and place them on the kitchen table. In fact, she would look for more makeshift vases and adorn each little room with color.

As she began to put some honest-to-goodness elbow grease into her work, her heart lifted to a brand-new high, and she found herself humming a happy tune.

If she closed her eyes, she could almost pretend she'd finally found a place to call home.

Jared kept busy for several hours, washing the windows inside and out. It had taken him two go-arounds to get the bulk of the dirt and grime cleaned up, and he figured one more time ought to do the trick.

Still, his stomach was growling and he was ready for a snack. So he entered the kitchen, where he found Sabrina seated on the faded linoleum, taking pots and pans out from the cupboard nearest the stove.

"I thought I'd head back to the house for a minute. Need anything?" His words pierced the silence, causing her to gasp and jump. She sure was a touchy little thing, and quick to respond.

In spite of himself and what he'd meant to be an innocent assessment of her nerves, "touchy" and "quick to respond" sent an entirely different message to his hormones.

"Actually," Sabrina said, "I could sure use some shelf paper and a pair of scissors, although I'm not sure if your mother has any she can spare."

"I'll see what I can find."

As Sabrina returned to her work, Jared headed for the ranch house, intent on getting more paper towels, too. He also meant to get them something to eat. He probably should have asked Sabrina if there was something particular that she was hungry for, but decided to surprise her instead.

Twenty minutes later, he returned with a box in his arms that bore the items she'd requested, as well as lunch for two.

"I'm back," he said from the cabin door, thinking he ought to give her a heads-up. When he walked into the kitchen, he realized giving her fair warning had been a good idea.

She'd climbed on a chair and was washing out the inside of one of the kitchen cupboards. She turned to greet him with a smile, and he noticed that she had a smudge of dirt on her forehead and a strand of dark hair had loosened from her braid and now lay along her cheek.

He wondered if she knew. Probably not. And he wouldn't tell her. He actually liked to see her a bit mussed. It made her seem real, and he could almost imagine her completely trustworthy.

"I brought lunch, too." He placed the box on the table, which appeared to be clean. "I thought you might be hungry. Why don't you stop and take a break?"

When he glanced over his shoulder, he found her watching him from atop the chair. Then she cocked her head and touched her bottom lip. "What's that on your face? It looks like chocolate."

"It probably is." He shrugged, then swiped at his mouth with the back of his hand. "No one was in the kitchen, so I finished off the cake while I had a chance."

Sabrina climbed down from the chair, then washed her hands at the sink and dried them. "I hope Connie has something else to serve as dessert tonight."

"Me, too. Especially since more than one of us are

making meals out of her sweets." Jared pulled out the shelf paper and scissors from his box, then set them on the counter. Next he removed sandwiches, a Thermos and two glasses.

"Thanks for thinking about me." Sabrina joined Jared at the table.

"I brought iced tea to drink," he said as he set everything out, using sheets of paper towels as place mats. "It's sweetened. I hope that's okay."

"It's perfect." Sabrina glanced at her watch. "Oh. It's already after one. No wonder I'm hungry."

"Everyone else at the house had meat loaf, so count yourself lucky to get a ham sandwich."

"I take it that meat loaf isn't one of your favorites."

"It's okay. I don't normally mind it, but Connie could really use some cooking lessons. Or maybe she just needs to pay more attention to the stove timer. That meat loaf looked pretty dry." He handed Sabrina a paper cup filled with iced tea, trying to get some of the ice cubes into her glass. "So what's her story? Obviously Connie isn't a chef by trade. But I figure it was the only job Granny had left to offer."

"You might be right. I don't know Connie very well. She's pretty quiet and keeps to herself. I think she's probably very shy."

"Where did she meet Granny?"

"At the doctor's office in town. Connie had fainted while sitting in the waiting room, and when Granny overheard her say that she needed a job and a place to stay, she offered her both. Connie hasn't been living here very long."

Jared unwrapped his sandwich, hoping whatever ill-

ness Connie had contracted was no longer contagious.
All they needed was an epidemic on the ranch. "What
was wrong with her?"

"Nothing really." Sabrina peeked under the top slice
of bread, then covered it back up. "She's pregnant and
had morning sickness when she first arrived, but that
seems to have passed now."

Jared fought off a curse. Doc had mentioned one of
the women might be pregnant.

What was Granny going to do with a baby under-
foot?

Besides that, the house was packed as it was. So
even if Sabrina moved out to the cabin, it wouldn't help
the overcrowding for very long.

If anything, Jared was further convinced that he
needed to run off the freeloaders, pack up his mother
and take her back to his ranch so he could take care of
her. She was only going to get older and more vulnerable.

He took a bite of his sandwich. While he chewed, he
scanned the kitchen, noting the progress Sabrina had
made. There'd been some, he suspected. But not
enough. "Have you had a chance to see if everything is
in good working order in here?"

"The oven doesn't heat, but I can get by without it
for a while."

"I'll take a look at it. Maybe I can fix it. I'm going
to need some new faucets for the bathroom, as well as
some valves and a P-trap. I plan to go to the hardware
store in town and pick up parts and supplies later today.
So if I need anything for the stove or oven, I can get
them while I'm out." Jared slowly shook his head. "See?

I told you it would take a lot to whip this place into shape."

Sabrina slid him an easy smile. "You're probably right, but I don't mind the work. It's actually...kind of fun."

He couldn't help but take another note of the smudge on her forehead and the loose strand of hair that fell near her ear. Yet a gleam in her eyes suggested that she meant every word she said.

"And you're actually happy to move in here?" Not that he was trying to talk her out of it.

"Absolutely."

"That surprises me."

"Why?"

"Because something tells me you're used to so much more."

"Then that *something* is lying to you."

Was she pulling his leg?

"You seem so prim and proper, Sabrina. So tidy. It's hard to believe you weren't brought up in the lap of luxury."

She lifted a delicate brow, which placed a furrow right through the dirty spot on her face. "I'm not sure if I should thank you or not. Either way, things were never easy for me or my brother. My parents were little more than kids themselves when my mom got pregnant—and not with just one baby but two. So we spent our early years moving from one place to another."

"You mean, you were raised in foster care?" Like me? he wondered.

"No. Our parents moved with us. At first, we bounced back and forth between our grandparents' houses. But our mom and dad both came from big families, so there was never a lot of room. And then things would always get…weird. Or awkward. And we'd have to leave."

"How long did that go on?"

"Let's just say that whenever we wore out our welcome at one place, we'd move to another. Living out of boxes didn't seem to faze my parents or even my twin brother. But I guess, by nature, I crave stability."

And her brother, the trucker, didn't? Talk about not having a place to lay his head at night.

Jared wanted to quiz her about Carlos, Joey's dad, but he didn't. There was still so much about *her* he had to learn. Yet, sometimes, her answers just left him with more questions.

She set her half-eaten sandwich aside. "When I was a little girl, I tried my best to control my life and organize my environment, but it was almost impossible to do."

"So you're trying to make up for that now at work by filing everything carefully and keeping the office in order?"

She smiled wistfully. "Actually, it's been an ongoing thing for me. I remember one of my teachers telling my mom that she'd never seen a child with such a neat and organized desk. She went on to say that she wished all of her students were that responsible."

Jared took a swig of iced tea, letting it wash down the last of his sandwich. If Connie hadn't overcooked the ham a bit too much, it might have tasted better. But it had to beat the heck out of that meat loaf.

He turned his attention back to Sabrina and the story

she'd been telling him. "Did your folks ever find a permanent place of their own?"

"They divorced when Carlos and I were eight, and the moves merely continued. First we lived with my mom and her boyfriend. Then with my dad and his new wife."

"I did a lot of moving around when I was a kid," Jared admitted. "And it sucked. It was hard to make friends. Or to give a damn about going to school."

"You're right. But in spite of the constant upheavals, I survived. I also studied hard."

"Don't tell me. Let me guess. You found an aptitude for math, a subject with rules and properties that remained constant. And so you decided to become a number cruncher and put that skill to use."

She lifted her glass and took a sip. "That's about the size of it. I was determined not to make the same mistakes my parents made—like getting pregnant too soon or married too young."

She was still young now. Early twenties, he suspected.

"Does that mean you don't date very much?" He wasn't sure why he asked, why he cared.

She paused and bit down on her bottom lip, as though trying to decide how much she wanted to confess. "I guess you could say that. I've had boyfriends, but when they realized I wasn't going to risk getting physically involved, things sort of fizzled out."

Did that mean she was a virgin?

He found the possibility…intriguing. And somewhat challenging. That is, if he wanted to risk getting physically involved with a woman he wasn't yet sure he could trust.

"When my brother was sixteen," Sabrina said, "he and his girlfriend weren't as careful as they should have been, and she got pregnant. When I saw what he and Suzy went through, I was even more determined to focus on the future, rather than the here and now."

"So Carlos got married young?"

"No. He claimed he wasn't in love with Suzy, although I don't believe that. Instead I think he was afraid of repeating family history."

Jared tensed, not liking the thought of a man who refused to take responsibility for his mistakes. After all, Carlos was off driving big rigs across the country, and his sister was stuck raising the kid he'd fathered.

Not that Joey was a problem child. He was polite, appreciative and nice to be around. It was obvious that he craved a father's attention, though. And that made Jared feel sorry for him.

Sabrina must have sensed Jared's disapproval because she added, "My brother dropped out of school and went to work so that he could pay child support. But he didn't think he was old enough to know what love really was and didn't want to make a commitment he couldn't keep."

As far as Jared was concerned, her brother had an unspoken commitment to his son the moment he'd been conceived. Fathers weren't supposed to walk away from their kids, leaving them for someone else to raise.

A piece of lettuce dropped out of Sabrina's sandwich and onto the paper towel. She picked it up and popped it into her mouth.

"But what about now?" Jared said. "Joey needs him."

"Yes, I know, but…"

"Your brother ought to find another job and stay home."

"You don't understand. Carlos has...reasons why he can't do that."

"What are they?"

She didn't answer right away, and for a moment he wondered if she would. Finally, she said, "I don't feel right discussing them with you. You'll just have to believe me when I say that for the past seven years I've felt sorry for all of them—Carlos, Suzy and Joey."

"Okay," he said. "We'll leave it at that. But surely there was someone other than you who could have stepped up to the plate."

"Suzy's family...well, they weren't much help. And to be honest, none of the relatives on either side were willing or able to take him, so it was up to me. I put my schooling on hold to take care of Joey."

"You gave up college?"

"I'll go back someday."

Her tone lacked all but a spark of determination, and he suspected that she might not be so sure about that.

"Besides," she added, "Joey was closer to me than to anyone else. And I love him like my own. There really wasn't any question about who would be the best one to take him."

"And now you're here," he said.

"Yes. And since your mother offered me a place to stay and let me bring Joey, it seemed to solve most of my immediate problems."

Her gaze snagged his, and something twisted in his chest. Something that had been ramrod straight and as tough as cowhide.

All right. So the story she'd shared had touched him, just as it must have done to his mom.

But did it also give Sabrina a motive to steal?

The next morning, as Jared stood on the porch scanning the dark clouds that were gathering overhead, Hilda Detweiler, an old friend of Granny's, drove into the yard in a red '86 Cadillac Seville, parking only steps away from the front porch.

Hilda used to own and operate the Pampered Lady Beauty Parlor in Brighton Valley, but sold it about fifteen years ago and retired. To this day, she continued to work part-time out of her home, though, fixing the hair of some of her oldest and best customers.

Granny was one of them.

For as long as Jared could remember, and probably decades longer than that, Hilda and Granny had been good friends. Each Sunday morning, they spent the day in town, where they attended church, had lunch at Darla's Diner and then either went shopping or to a movie.

The perfectly coiffed silver-haired lady rolled down the window of her car. "Why, Jared Clayton. Aren't you a sight for poor eyes."

"Good morning, Hilda," Jared said. "I see you and Granny are off to church."

"At our age, your mother and I figure we ought to watch our spiritual p's and q's. You never know when we'll find ourselves standing at the Pearly Gates, hoping someone will recognize us and invite us inside."

Before Jared could do much more than chuckle, Granny walked out the front door, dressed in a pair of pink slacks, a white blouse and a sweater. A white leather handbag and a black raincoat dangled from the crook of her arm. "Are you sure you don't want to go with us, son? That new preacher isn't half-bad. And better yet, he's not as long-winded as the old one."

"Not this time," Jared said, providing the same response he always gave her whenever she invited him to church. "You two go on. I've got some work to do out at the cabin."

"That's good to hear." Granny grinned, eyes twinkling. "I sure appreciate you helping Sabrina. That little gal has taken on a huge chore. The cabin was nearly falling apart when Clem died."

She had *that* right.

Late yesterday afternoon, Jared had driven to town and picked up the lumber, parts and supplies he needed at Riley's Hardware Store. All the while, Sabrina had stayed behind and continued to work.

By the time he'd unpacked everything at the cabin, it was already dusk, and he'd had to convince her to quit for the day. Since the lighting wasn't that good, she'd been forced to agree. But then she'd spent the evening washing towels and sheets she'd found in the cupboards.

He wondered if the physical labor had helped her sleep better last night, suspecting so. He hadn't heard a peep out of her after the washing machine finally finished its last spin cycle and shut down.

As Granny climbed into the car, Jared told Hilda to drive carefully. "The weather report says there's a storm heading our way."

"It's not supposed to hit until this afternoon," Hilda said. "We'll be back by then."

Jared nodded, then strode toward the cabin, intent on

repairing the porch before the rain came. As he approached, he found the front door open wide.

"Sabrina?" he called.

"I'm in the bathroom," she answered.

He made his way inside, where he found her bent over the tub, scouring out a rust spot that wasn't likely to recede. The denim stretched and molded around her hips, offering him a view that sent his testosterone levels surging and damn near pumped him full of ideas he had no business having.

She turned and cast him a smile. "Good morning."

"You're up early," he said. Bright-eyed and bushy-tailed came to mind, but he wouldn't go there.

"I wanted to get as much done today as I could. There's a chance we could move in this evening."

"There's an even bigger chance of rain," Jared said. "So moving may have to wait until tomorrow."

She shrugged. "Well, I can hope, can't I?"

"You're really eager to get out of the house."

Her expression sobered. "It's not as though I'm not grateful for the room we were given—"

"I know." At least, he thought he did—if the story she'd told him had been true. Still, he was certain she'd been holding something back about her brother, and that didn't sit well with him. But he tossed her a crooked grin anyway.

He supposed she'd read sincerity and compassion in his response, because the pretty smile she threw back at him shot straight through his chest, knocking him off balance.

"I...uh..." He nodded toward the tub, wanting—no, needing—to put some distance between the two of them. "I'd better mend that porch and let you get busy, or this place will never be ready."

"You know," she said, cheeks flushing a pretty shade of pink, "I didn't think much of you when I first met you. But I was wrong."

He hadn't thought much of her, either. And he still had a hard time believing she was everything she appeared to be—a loyal sister, a loving aunt, a dedicated and honest employee.

For cripe's sake, she even implied that she was a virgin. But Jared didn't take anyone at face value anymore.

He'd been burned by one pretty face already.

## Chapter Six

A couple of hours later, Jared had repaired the porch, changed a few light switches and replaced the bathroom plumbing. Sabrina had kept busy, too, which made it easy for him to stay out of her way.

At least, until she called out his name.

"Jared? Will you please come here? I need your help."

He followed her voice into the bedroom, where she stood beside the bare mattress and box springs of a queen-size bed, hands on her hips.

"I stripped this down yesterday and washed all the linen, so I'd like to make it back up again. But first, can you help me turn the mattress and move the bed against the other wall?"

"Sure."

Two pairs of hands made it an easy task.

"Thank you," Sabrina said. "Not just for this, but for all your help with the cabin. You've been a godsend."

He didn't know about that. "You're welcome, but I think it's only fair to tell you that my motives are purely selfish. The sooner you can move in here, the sooner I can get off the sofa in the den."

A smile dimpled her cheeks and added a sparkle to her eyes. "Well, I can't fault you for being honest."

"Hey," a small voice called from the open front door. "Sabrina? Are you in there?"

"Come on in, Joey." Sabrina left the bedroom, with Jared bringing up the rear like a little lapdog.

Of course, he had to admit that following behind Sabrina had its perks, like being able to watch the way her shapely hips swayed with each step she took.

As they neared the living room, he tore his gaze from the sexy view of Sabrina's backside, focusing on her nephew instead. Joey held a brown sack in his hand as he carefully scanned the interior of the cabin.

"What do you think?" Sabrina asked the boy.

"You were right. It's *really* cool." He beamed as though he'd entered a mansion. "Wow. We get a fireplace and a TV, *too*."

Jared hoped the television worked. And that the antenna was still receiving. Every once in a while, after a strong wind, Clem would have to climb on the roof and readjust it so it would pick up a strong signal.

"What have you got there?" Sabrina asked the child.

Joey glanced at the bag. "Oh, you mean, this? Connie wanted me to bring it to you."

Lunch? Jared wondered. If it was, that was too bad. He'd planned to go back to the house and rustle up something for him and Sabrina to eat—something Connie hadn't made. But apparently, he should have done that sooner.

Sabrina took the brown sack from him. "What's in here?"

"Apple stu… Apple stru…"

"Strudel?"

He nodded. "Yeah, that's it. Connie made a whole bunch this morning because everyone loves her dessert so much that they've been sneaking the leftovers."

Sabrina pulled out a foil-wrapped container and three plastic baggies. One was filled with coffee grounds, another with sugar and the last one held what appeared to be instant creamer. "How thoughtful of her."

If the strudel tasted as good as her cakes and cookies, the gesture would be appreciated by everyone who had to depend upon Connie for sustenance, especially Jared.

"Joey," Sabrina said, "why don't you come with me into the kitchen? I'm going to cut this into three pieces so we can share it."

"Oh, that's okay." The boy rubbed his stomach. "I ate two helpings already. Connie just told me to bring that to you. But I gotta hurry back. Me and Tori and Connie are playing Go Fish. It's a really cool game."

Jared could see that it didn't take much to make the boy happy: a ride on the horse; a fifteen-year-old television in a run-down cabin; a card game.

"Okay," his aunt said. "I don't want to keep you from having fun."

Joey turned and dashed out the door, obviously in a hurry to get back to the house. He sure seemed to like it on the Rocking C.

How could he not?

Jared had been a city kid, too, and he'd thrived in a ranch environment. Of course, it had been more than just the wide-open spaces, the cows and the horses. There'd also been a masculine camaraderie, too. Clem and the other cowboys had taken Jared under wing, making him one of them and filling the empty gap in his life that his old man had left. They'd taught him everything he knew about roping and riding and being a man. And lessons like that couldn't be bought.

Jared's thoughts drifted to Joey, who'd mentioned how much he'd like to learn how to ride a horse all by himself. The conversation they'd shared replayed in his mind.

*But Aunt Sabrina won't let me ask anyone here at the ranch to teach me,* he'd said. *She doesn't want us to wear out our welcome.*

If that were the case, then maybe, one day soon, Jared would surprise the boy by saddling up one of the old mares and giving him a couple of tips about horses and riding. That ought to really slap a smile on his face.

And maybe, after a couple of weeks on the ranch, Joey would bulk up and get some color in his cheeks.

"Mmm," Sabrina said, drawing Jared's attention. She held the foil-wrapped package under her nose and closed her eyes. "This strudel smells so good. And it's still warm. I'm going to put on a pot of coffee to go with it. Are you ready to take a break?"

"Sounds good to me."

"Good. If you don't mind, I'll finish making up the bed first."

He watched as she left the room, hips swaying in a mesmerizing fashion.

Damn. He was going to have to watch his growing fascination with her backside.

A light lit the cabin like a camera flash, and moments later, thunder rumbled in the distance. There was a chill in the air, he realized. One he hadn't noticed earlier.

He made his way to the window and peered outside. The sky had grown dark and threatening, especially in the east. The weatherman had been right when he'd predicted rain, but it looked as though it was moving in sooner than expected.

If Sabrina actually planned to move in later this afternoon, it might be a good idea to make a trek to the woodpile and start a fire in the hearth. So he strode to the side of the barn, where the wood was stacked, and loaded up an armload. It took him several trips to get enough to last her through the night.

He had no more than stacked the last piece on the porch, when Sabrina let out a scream that nearly blew off the roof.

Damn. What in the hell happened?

A shot of adrenaline raced through him, and he ran to the kitchen.

Had she sliced her hand open while trying to cut into the strudel?

He found her crawling on the table, her eyes open wide, her complexion pale.

"What's the matter?"

She pointed into the corner near the fridge. "A mouse. A big one. It ran across my foot and scared me half to death."

His heart was pounding so hard it damn near jumped out of his chest. "Is that all?"

"What do you mean, *is that all?*" She shuddered. "They're…ooh." She pushed up from the tabletop with her hands, straightening until she was kneeling and her bottom was resting on her heels. Then she shimmied in fright. "I hate mice."

"I can't understand why. Those little things won't hurt you."

"I don't care. I can't even stand the sight of them."

"You've convinced me of that. But you'd better get down from that table. It's not very sturdy, and if it collapses with you on it, you'll be at a real disadvantage. With a broken neck or leg, you won't be able to escape the little critter."

"We'll need to set traps. Lots of them. No matter how badly I want to move in, I can't stay in here with a mouse."

Jared had a feeling that there was more than one small, furry varmint taking up residence in the cabin. But what did she expect? This building was old, and the field mice had probably been nesting in it for years.

"I wouldn't worry about it," he said. "I have a feeling that little critter is on its last legs."

"You think it's dying?" She scrunched her face. "No way. That thing looked as healthy as a horse."

"Maybe, but that banshee scream you let out was loud enough to chase every animal within a hundred-mile radius to go charging into the Gulf of Mexico." He slowly shook his head, then reached for her. "Come on. Get down. You probably don't weigh much more than a hundred pounds, but that table has always been wobbly."

She scanned the floor, no doubt looking to make sure the mouse was long gone, then let him help her.

He placed his hands around her waist, then swung her around. As he did so, she slid down the front of him. The buttons of their shirts clicked against each other, but all he could think of was the way her breasts splayed against his chest, how their hearts beat warm and vibrant.

How he wished their clothing hadn't stood in the way.

He could have let her go and stepped aside. In fact, he *should* have.

But as their gazes locked, so did their arms—his around her waist, hers on his shoulders.

Something powerful snaked around them, something far more threatening—and imminent—than the storm on the horizon.

Sabrina's lips parted as though she was just as aware of what was going to happen as he was. And just as powerless to stop it.

Every lick of sense Jared had ever possessed, every ounce of self-control, deserted him as he drew her close and lowered his mouth to hers.

He took it slow and easy at first, his lips brushing hers gently, but when she slid her arms around his neck and lifted up on tiptoe for a better reach, he was lost in a surge of heat and desire.

A sense of urgency swept over him, and he drew her close. He felt a growing compulsion to run his fingers through her long, silky hair, something he'd been dying to do ever since he'd seen it loose that first night. But she'd woven it into a braid again today, so he had to be content with what he did have access to—her sweet, willing mouth.

She'd implied that she had very little experience with

this sort of thing, but that sure as hell didn't seem to be the case right now. And as much as he'd wanted to keep his distance from her, he lost that fight and savored one of the most arousing kisses he'd ever had.

She tasted of apples and cinnamon, no doubt from a bite of strudel she'd snagged for herself moments earlier, and he couldn't seem to get his fill of her sweetness.

But he might have, if a flash of lighting and a subsequent boom of thunder hadn't rolled across the Texas sky.

He drew back, mourning what they'd shared instantly, yet knowing how crazy it had been to lose his head like that. He wanted to apologize. Or to laugh it off. To make an excuse that would turn back the clock and put them both on an even keel. But he couldn't think of a damn thing to say.

Her lips, still plump and rosy from the assault of his mouth, parted. Apparently, when it came to conjuring some kind of verbal response, she was in the same quandary as he was. So he decided to make it easy on her—and on himself—by pretending the kiss had never happened.

"Why don't you start the coffee while I get a fire going," he said.

Trouble was, it was hotter than hell in the cabin already, and he hadn't even struck a match.

Sabrina, her mind still numb from the intoxicating kiss she and Jared had shared, struggled through the steps of making coffee in an old, electric percolator she'd found while cleaning the cupboards yesterday.

As she inserted the plug into an outlet near the counter, she trailed her fingers over her lips, amazed that a man's mouth and tongue could make her feel so weak-kneed and dreamy.

Never had she been held so close, kissed so thoroughly, and something told her she would never experience the like again. Not that she was any kind of expert on kissing or sex. But she *was* human.

And her hormones had certainly been in good working order today.

She tried to keep her mind occupied with thoughts of anything other than Jared, but she couldn't seem to focus, not even on the brewing coffee, something she'd been craving earlier.

Unfortunately, she was craving something entirely different now.

But kissing her employer's son had certainly been a complication she hadn't planned on. Of course, he lived nearly a hundred miles away and was only here temporarily, so nothing would become of it anyway. Still, it hadn't been a wise or professional thing to do.

Yet as much as she knew better than to ever let herself get in that position, she feared that when faced with another opportunity to kiss Jared, she might be tempted to do it again.

She shot a glance at the refrigerator, where the pesky mouse had run.

Had Jared been right? Had her scream frightened the little creature to death?

Surely not. But maybe it had scurried outside, trying to find a safe place to hide. She hoped so. She couldn't handle seeing it again.

Either way, the sooner she could get out of the kitchen, the better.

As Clem's old percolator whished out one long, last burble, indicating the coffee was finally done, Sabrina glanced at the kitchen window and saw that the rain had begun to pelt the glass.

From in the living room, she could smell the fire in the hearth.

She both dreaded and looked forward to facing Jared again. But there was no way around it, she supposed. After removing the built-in cutting board from the counter, she covered it with a paper towel and used it as a tray to carry the plates of strudel, cups of coffee, sugar and cream into the living room.

Jared, who'd been kneeling by the hearth, staring as the flames licked the logs, turned and stood as she entered the room.

"Need some help?" he asked.

"Thanks, but I've got it under control." She set the cutting board on the lamp table. "How do you like your coffee?"

"Black."

She nodded, then handed him a cup and took a seat on the sofa. He joined her, leaving a physical gap between them, but not nearly as pronounced as the invisible one that the kiss had created.

The warm, flickering fire, the aroma of fresh-brewed coffee and the taste of apples and cinnamon made the little cabin feel much cozier and warmer than Sabrina had ever imagined it could be, yet she was still on edge and not sure what to say.

Bringing up that kiss certainly wasn't something she

was willing to do, so she chose a subject that was easier to discuss. "Do you know if Mrs. Clayton—or rather your mother—returned Wayne Templeton's call yet?"

"Who's he?"

"I'm not sure exactly." Sabrina added creamer and sugar to her coffee. "He said that he's with Dazzling Desert Ventures."

Jared took a sip from his mug before setting it aside and reaching for a plate of strudel. "When did he call?"

"On Friday. I passed the message on to her, and she said she wanted to run something by you and Matt about it first. So I was just curious, that's all."

"She never said a word to me." Jared used his fork to break off a bite-size portion of the dessert. "But if it's the guy who wants to buy that property, I'm a little worried about her negotiating a land deal, especially with a company called Dazzling Desert Ventures."

"I suppose it could have been a telemarketer trying to sell her a time-share or something."

"It's possible. But maybe I ought to call the guy back. Did you keep a record of his number?"

"Yes. In the office."

They ate in silence, each deep in thought. But Sabrina suspected it was more than real estate that had Jared so quiet.

Just as it was for her.


The coffee break didn't last long, and after another hour of work in the cabin, the rain slowed to a sprinkle.

"There seems to be a lull in the storm," Jared said, "although I don't expect it to last long. Maybe we ought to head back to the house while we have a chance to stay dry."

Sabrina agreed, so they sloshed through the water-soaked yard and entered through the mudroom, where Jared kicked off his boots and Sabrina left her shoes.

In the kitchen, Connie stood over the stove, frying up chicken, while Tori sat at the table with a coffee mug in front of her. They'd been chatting, but their conversation suddenly stilled, which made Jared wonder whether they were conspiring about something.

He glanced at a platter filled with golden-brown chicken—legs, thighs, breasts. Had Tori been giving Connie cooking lessons? If so, he didn't mind them being in cahoots about that.

"Thanks for sending Joey with the coffee and strudel," Sabrina told Connie. "It was delicious. And a real treat."

"You're welcome. I thought you might need a break."

"We did, so your timing was perfect." Sabrina looked toward the doorway that led to the rest of the house. "Where's Joey?"

"He's watching a cartoon on television in the family room," Tori said. "I know you're careful about what he can see, so I made sure it was appropriate."

It was a good thing Jared didn't have to make decisions about what was appropriate for kids to do or see. He wasn't up on current child-rearing practices, and since Jolene hadn't wanted to have a baby, he hadn't given it any thought.

"Your brother's in the living room," Tori told Jared.

"I hope he's behaving himself, too." Jared had meant his response to be tongue in cheek, as if Tori would have made sure Matt, like Joey, was involved in some kind of age-appropriate activity.

"Has your brother always been grumpy?" the redheaded maid asked. "Or did his attitude change after the accident?"

Jared didn't normally like discussing his brother's depression with anyone other than one of the doctors, but he figured a truthful answer wasn't going to hurt. Yet it didn't take a board of surgeons to see that Matt could be an ass, whether he had reason to be or not. "He lost someone he cared about in that accident. And he's had to give up a career in the rodeo. I can't really blame him for being miserable."

"The poor man," Tori said. "Maybe I ought to talk to him."

Jared wasn't sure what she could say that would help. But he figured it wouldn't hurt if she tried. Matt might look vulnerable, but he'd always been scrappy and strong-willed. In fact, in some ways, he was probably even more so now.

"Well," Tori said, getting to her feet and carrying her cup to the sink. "I'd better get back to work. My coffee break is over."

As she left the kitchen, Connie, who'd been listening intently to the conversation, turned back to the stove and sucked in a breath. "Oh, darn it. Now, these are going to be extra-crispy and a bit on the dark side."

Apparently, the new cook was easily distracted and did a better job when she was able to throw a dessert into a preset oven and not pay it any mind until the timer went off.

Jared turned his attention to Sabrina. "When you get a chance, will you please get me Wayne's number?"

"I'll get it now," she said. "For what it's worth it had a 702 area code."

Jared had called Jolene enough times to know the guy was calling from Nevada. "It must be the man who wants to buy her property."

"That's what I was thinking," Sabrina said. "If you'll excuse me, I'll be right back."

Jared followed her as far as the living room, where the front door suddenly swung open and Granny stepped inside. Once she'd shut out the dreary weather, she whistled out a "Whew."

"You're home earlier than usual," Jared said.

Granny wiped her feet on the rug in the entry, then shucked off her black coat. "That's because Hilda doesn't like driving in the rain anymore. And I can't say as I blame her. When you're our age, the damp weather is tough on the bones and joints."

"Mrs. Clayton," Sabrina said, "did you ever get a chance to call Mr. Templeton or talk to your sons about him?"

Matt glanced up, his brow furrowed. "Who's he?"

"Wayne Templeton is one of the fellows who are interested in the property in Nevada. He wanted to know if I received the offer he mailed me the other day." Granny hung her coat on the hook by the door, then shuffled into the living area and took a seat on the sofa.

"You got an offer?" Jared asked.

"Yes. Hilda and I picked it up from my post-office box while we were in Brighton Valley. And to tell you the truth, I'd just as soon sell it. What do I need a bunch of cacti and scrub brush for?"

"Before selling it, I think someone ought to fly out to Las Vegas and see just where it's located." Jared leaned his side against the backrest of the recliner and crossed his arms.

"Good idea." Granny smiled at Sabrina. "I'll give you power of attorney and let you handle the deal with those casino bigwigs."

"Now, wait a minute," Jared said, straightening. "You can't just send her out there alone."

"Why not?" Granny asked.

Because that "desert property" could be worth a hell of a lot more than either Granny or Sabrina imagined. And if a casino was interested in it… Hell, if that were the case, neither one of those women were prepared to negotiate a deal of that type.

Jared would insist upon going to Las Vegas for Granny and leaving Sabrina behind, but with both women eyeing him as though he'd just walked into the room buck naked, he figured he'd better be careful how he worded it.

"I have a friend who's a real-estate attorney in Vegas," Jared explained. "I'll call in a favor and ask his opinion on the deal."

"Fine," Granny said. "Then you and Sabrina can both go on my behalf."

Together?

That hadn't been what Jared had in mind.

"Actually," Sabrina said, "I really don't want to drag Joey to Las Vegas."

Jared felt the tension slip off his shoulders. Good. He'd much rather handle this on his own.

"Don't you worry one little bit about Joey." Granny grinned and eased back into the comfort of the sofa cushions. "I'll watch him. And Tori and Connie will help me."

Jared stole a glance at Sabrina, who appeared to be just as surprised by the travel arrangements as he was. But he figured there wasn't anything either of them could do or say to change Granny's mind when she got something wedged in it.

And apparently, she was dead set on being represented by both of them.

"Well," he said, wondering how Sabrina felt about all of this and taking a good, hard look at his mother, "I guess you've made up your mind."

Granny beamed, as if she had it all aced—the deal and the sale.

Jared's gaze drifted to Sabrina. As their eyes met and locked, something rushed between them. Something breathless and hot.

It was just the memory of the kiss, he supposed. And the thought of a repeat.

But, hey. What happened in Vegas, stayed in Vegas.

## Chapter Seven

On Monday morning, Jared entered the kitchen after the men had gone to start their chores. He drank a cup of coffee and munched on a couple of pieces of toast, then grabbed an apple from the fruit bowl on the table and went outside.

The sky was smudged and spotted with gray clouds, remnants of yesterday's storm, but the rain had passed. That was a good thing, he supposed, since he and Sabrina would be leaving today.

The first afternoon flight out of Houston that still had seats available didn't depart for Las Vegas until one o'clock, so there was no need to leave the ranch until nine.

For that reason, Jared stepped off the porch and headed for the barn, where he found Lester just outside his office, lighting up a cigarette.

"Got a minute?" he asked the lanky, weathered ranch foreman.

"Sure." Lester pulled a long drag, no doubt savoring the taste of tobacco, then blew it out. "What can I do for ya?"

"I'm looking for a dependable horse for Joey to ride while he's here. You got any suggestions?"

Lester stroked his chin, fingers brushing two-day-old whiskers, and gave it some thought.

Jared, who still held the apple he'd picked up in the house, rubbed it on his flannel shirt, giving it a shine, rather than a bite.

"You know," Lester said, "I've got a couple that might work out. Let me show 'em to you."

Five minutes and three horses later, they settled on Smokey, a sure-footed black gelding that had done his share of ranch work over the years, but was ready for an easier life. Smokey didn't know it, but he'd won a short reprieve from the auction block.

Jared thanked Lester, letting the foreman get back to work. Then he strode across the yard, making his way to the house. He spotted the boy seated on the steps leading to the mudroom.

Joey lifted his hand and wiggled his fingers in a fluttery wave. "Hi, Mr. Clayton."

"Well, now." A slow smile stretched across Jared's face. "You're just the guy I was looking for. I have something I need you to do for me."

The boy jumped to his feet. "Sure, Mr. Clayton. What is it?"

"We've got an old horse that needs someone to take care of him, and most of the cowboys are too busy to give him the kind of attention he needs."

"A *horse?*" The boy's voice was laced with awe. "A *real* one? And you need *me* to take care of him?"

"Absolutely. His name is Smokey. He's getting on in years and has pretty much been retired. But he was one of the best cutting horses we ever had. And it just doesn't seem fair for him to be stuck in a corral most of the day." Okay, so he'd stretched the truth, lending a bit more importance to the old black gelding's job on the ranch than was the case.

"What do you want me to do?" Joey asked.

"Well, it's probably a good idea for you to get to know him first, I suppose. You might start by talking to him and giving him some oats or chunks of carrots." Jared glanced at the apple in his hand, deciding on a better use for it than a snack before leaving for the airport. "Smokey was one heck of a good horse, so he deserves to be treated well. And something tells me you'd do right by him."

"Oh, I *will*. I'll take super good care of him."

"Come with me." Jared put the apple into his left hand and slid the right one into the front pocket of his jeans, withdrawing his Swiss Army knife. "Let's go meet him."

They walked toward the corral where the black gelding had been penned with a piebald mare.

"Which one is Smokey?" Joey asked.

"The biggest one." Jared whistled, and Smokey perked up his ears, but remained where he was standing.

"It looks like he's not too sure about us." Jared opened up his knife, then pared off a small chunk. "We're going to have to bribe him a little."

Slowly but surely, Smokey plodded toward the fence, where the man and boy waited.

# PLAY THE
# Lucky Key Game

## and you can get

**Do You Have the LUCKY KEY?**

# FREE BOOKS
## and FREE GIFTS!

*Scratch the gold areas with a coin. Then check below to see the books and gifts you can get!*

**YES!** I have scratched off the gold areas. Please send me the 2 FREE BOOKS and 2 FREE GIFTS, worth about $10, for which I qualify. I understand I am under no obligation to purchase any books, as explained on the back of this card.

**335 SDL ERT7**          **235 SDL ERXV**

|  |
|  |

FIRST NAME          LAST NAME

ADDRESS

APT.#          CITY

STATE / PROV.          ZIP/POSTAL CODE

www.eHarlequin.com

2 free books plus 2 free gifts          1 free book

2 free books          Try Again!

Offer limited to one per household and not valid to current subscribers of Silhouette Special Edition® books.
**Your Privacy** – Silhouette Books is committed to protecting your privacy. Our Privacy Policy is available online at www.eHarlequin.com or upon request from the Silhouette Reader Service. From time to time we make our lists of customers available to reputable third parties who may have a product or service of interest to you. If you would prefer for us not to share your name and address, please check here. ☐

"Here, Joey." Jared gave the child a piece of apple. "Hold your hand open flat. Like this. Keep your fingers out of the way and make Smokey do the work."

As the gelding sniffed, snorted then gobbled up the apple, the look of wonder that crossed Joey's face was priceless, and it released a flood of warmth in Jared's chest.

Was this how Clem had felt when he'd taken Jared under his wing years ago?

As the boy fed the horse another small piece of apple, the piebald figured out what was going on and tried to nose her way into the party.

Just like a female, Jared thought, as the memory of the night he'd first met Jolene settled over him.

He and his buddies, all Texas ranchers wearing Stetsons and boots, were kicking back and having a drink in one of the lounges in a prominent Las Vegas casino when she'd sidled up to the table.

"Is this seat taken?" she'd asked before claiming the one next to Jared. "I love cowboys."

If he'd realized the truth of her statement then and had known what the future would bring, he would have told her the seat wasn't available. It would have saved them both a hell of a lot of grief.

As Joey continued to feed the horses one small piece of apple after another, he giggled each time they nibbled against the palm of his hand.

The boy's delight made Jared chuckle, too, and he realized he was playing the same role in Joey's life—albeit temporarily—that Clem had once played in his. But, hey. That was okay. It seemed only right to pay it forward.

"You know," Jared said, "part of taking care of ol' Smokey will be to exercise him."

"How do I do that?"

"Well, you'll need to ride him, of course."

"*Ride* him?" The boy's eyes couldn't have grown any wider, his smile any broader. "Oh, wow. That would be *way* cool."

"I suppose I'll have to give you a few lessons, though. Can you wait until after my trip to Las Vegas?"

"If I have to." Joey bit on his bottom lip. "I mean, sure. I can wait."

"It would probably be a good idea if you came out and visited Smokey several times a day until I get back, though."

"Joey?" Sabrina called from the house.

"I'm over here," he yelled, before taking off at a run. He met his aunt before she could step a foot into the yard.

Jared followed behind at a normal pace, arriving in time to hear the boy try to catch his breath while blurting out, "Guess what? Mr. Clayton is showing me how to take care of a horse."

He went on to tell her about the important chore he'd been given, his excitement causing him to wheeze while spitting out the words.

"Take it easy there, sport." Jared grinned. "You're going to hyperventilate."

"What's that?" Joey asked, still huffing a bit.

"It's when you're talking so fast that you suck in too much air and can't catch your breath."

Had Jared been this excited when Clem and the other hands had taken him riding with them for the very first time?

He shook off a brief moment of concern and slid a glance at Sabrina, at the charcoal-gray business suit she wore. It was a shame she didn't wear skirts and dresses more often. She had a great pair of legs, and the khaki and denim pants she'd chosen before hadn't done them justice.

"Are you ready to go yet?" she asked him.

He was packed. But after taking a look at her, noticing how professional she looked, how carefully she'd dressed and applied her makeup, he had half a notion to stop in town and buy himself some new clothes. He'd only packed jeans and cotton shirts when he left his own ranch. But there was no reason to get fancy. Jared was more interested in meeting Wayne Templeton and letting the man think he was dealing with a run-of-the-mill cowboy and not a college-educated rancher.

Besides, it was always fun to mess with men who thought he was a hick.

As it was, Jared would let Sabrina be the one to go all out. He'd just enjoy having her on his arm. And in his sights.

Damn, she looked good.

A coat of mascara made her eyelashes long and luscious, setting off those pretty blue eyes. And the red lipstick she sported made her lips look plump and kissable. And the fact that he'd already had a taste of them only set his blood pumping and his hormones raging.

Her ebony hair, silky and soft, had been swept up into a neat professional twist. He'd love to see it again, flowing loosely down her back, love to run his fingers through the tresses.

Did she ever let her hair down during the daylight hours—literally or figuratively?

When she blessed Jared with a heart-stopping smile, the thought of their impending trip settled over him, and he couldn't shake a raw thrill himself. And not because he harbored any urges to return to the bright lights and excitement of Las Vegas.

He was actually looking forward to getting away with Sabrina—even if he was determined not to let things get out of hand.

As Sabrina made her way down the aisle of the plane, she scanned the interior of the cabin.

"There's row twelve," Jared said from behind her, his musky, mountain-fresh scent a blatant and stirring reminder of his masculine presence. "We're in D and E."

She looked at the stub of her boarding pass, then at the letters on the overhead compartment, realizing she had the middle seat.

"Are you okay with that?" he asked.

"Oh, sure. It's just that…" She shrugged one shoulder and offered him a wry smile. "It's my first time on an airplane, and I thought it might be nice to sit by the window so I could look out."

"No kidding? You've never flown before?"

She shook her head, then slid into her assigned seat and buckled up.

Jared, who had been pleased with his preferred spot next to the aisle, opened the overhead compartment and put their carry-on bags inside.

Then he sat next to Sabrina and asked, "Have you ever been to Las Vegas before?"

"No. Have you?"

"Yeah." He didn't offer an explanation, but as he

sobered, she got the feeling he was keeping something back. A gambling loss, maybe?

"It sounds as though the place might hold some bad memories," she said.

"You got that right."

She turned, studied his profile. "What happened?"

When he didn't answer right away, she began to wonder if she'd broached some big, dark secret he hadn't meant to share.

Finally, he blew out a sigh. "That's where I met my ex-wife."

"You're divorced?" Mrs. Clayton had mentioned that her boys were all single, so Sabrina had just assumed they'd never been married.

"Since last Christmas."

"I'm sorry."

"Don't be. The marriage didn't last very long. And we didn't have kids."

"Still…"

"It was no big deal—not the marriage or the divorce. I'm glad it's all over."

Was he?

As the flight attendant went over the safety features of the 737, Sabrina took note of the exits, hoping it wouldn't be necessary to know where they were and squelching a rising bit of nervousness.

Then, as the plane backed away from the gate and began to taxi, she realized no one was going to take the window seat next to her, which was nice. So she craned her neck to see the activity on the ground as the plane prepared to take off.

Fifteen minutes later, when the flight was underway,

she returned her attention to her ruggedly handsome traveling companion.

"So what was she like?" Sabrina asked.

"Who?"

"Your ex."

He shrugged. "Just like any old ex-wife, I suppose. Ugly, fat, toothless."

She caught a glimmer in his eye, although she wouldn't have believed him even if she'd suspected he was sincere. "That's not true."

"What makes you think that?"

"There had to have been something about the woman that attracted you to her."

"I was drunk when I met her."

She studied his profile, the high cheekbones, the square-cut jaw, looking for some indication that he was joking. She couldn't possibly imagine him with an unattractive woman. Of course, she wasn't particularly comfortable with the thought of him with a pretty one, either.

"I don't believe you," she finally said. "You couldn't have been that drunk."

"There were times after we split up that I questioned how sober I could have been. Otherwise, I had to wonder about both my intelligence and my sanity."

He made it sound as though there hadn't been any emotion involved. But somehow that was hard to believe. Men didn't have to get married for sex anymore. Not when it was so readily available. And Sabrina suspected Jared wouldn't have to go to any trouble at all to find someone ready, willing and able—without offering any promises.

So she concluded that, in spite of what he was telling her, the divorce couldn't have been that easy.

"Was the relationship that bad?"

"Not at first. But it was a mistake for us to get married. Looking back, I'm not sure why we did." He glanced away, across the aisle.

She sensed that he didn't want to talk about it, so she returned her attention to the window and the white, billowy clouds below them.

For the most part, the trip was uneventful, other than a bit of turbulence over the mountains. It didn't seem to faze either Jared or the flight attendants, who passed out drinks and small bags of peanuts. So Sabrina relaxed and enjoyed the view until the captain announced the plane had begun its descent.

As the flight attendants prepared for landing, Sabrina stole a glance at Jared and caught him studying her in a way that set her pulse racing.

She offered him a smile, yet wondered what had caused the intensity in his gaze.

Las Vegas memories he'd like to forget?

Anticipation of the land deal they'd be negotiating?

Or was it something about *her* that had caught his eye and had him deep in thought?

It was strange, but twice in one day Jared had been on hand to watch someone experience the thrill of doing something for the very first time—Joey feeding the gelding, and now Sabrina sitting beside him on an airplane, her delight almost palpable.

He'd found himself caught up in the excitement with each of them, even though horseback riding and air travel no longer seemed like a big deal to him. But that hadn't always been the case, and it was nice having the chance to relive that first-time buzz through their eyes.

"What's wrong?" Sabrina asked.

"Nothing."

There was something in her expression—skepticism, maybe, or sympathy?

"Really," he said. "There isn't anything wrong."

Not yet, anyway. She'd touched him in a way he wasn't used to, in a place he ought to keep out of reach.

He gave her a pat on her knee…it was bare, soft and warm. The boldness of his move surprised the hell out him, since it suggested an intimacy he hadn't wanted to share again.

"Are you sure it's nothing?" She cocked her head slightly to the side, compassion attempting to soothe him where he'd once been hurt and had already healed. "I get the feeling that something is bothering you. Memories of your ex, maybe."

"Jolene?" He shook his head. "Not at all. I'm not one to stew about a mistake I made in the heat of the moment."

"Good." Sabrina's scent, something floral and breezy, softened the business cut of her suit and proclaimed a gentle femininity a guy could really get used to.

Just sitting next to her was enough to make Jared question what he'd ever felt for Jolene. And to remind him of the heated kiss he and Sabrina had shared in the kitchen of Clem's cabin.

"By the way," he said, trying to steer the subject into safer water, "I called my friend last night. The attorney I mentioned?"

"The one you were going to consult with on the property sale?"

"Yes. His name is Steve Rankin. I gave him the parcel number of Granny's property, and faxed him a copy of the offer she received. He agreed to meet us at his office as soon as we arrive and promised to have some comps and more information for us."

"Good idea. At least we'll know what we're up against." She rested her elbow on the armrest, turning toward him. Taunting him with that lovely scent again.

So much for changing the subject and regaining his balance.

"Where did you meet Steve?" she asked.

"At Caesar's Palace about five years ago. We were sitting at the same blackjack table. He was at first base, and I was at third. Together, we made a pretty good team, and I think we each walked away with more than five grand. It made for a pleasant night."

"I bet." She grinned. "No pun intended."

He returned her smile. "Steve and I hit it off, and since we were both hungry, we had dinner together. When we found out we both went to Texas A&M, a friendship developed."

"I didn't know you went to college."

There was a lot about him she didn't know. "I nearly dropped out when Clem got sick, but he raised such a ruckus that I filed incompletes. And then he made me promise to go back and get a degree."

"Did you?"

"Yeah. So there's no reason why you can't do the same."

She nibbled her bottom lip, and her eyes seemed a bit glassy. "I know. I plan to."

Jared wasn't at all good at providing emotional support to a woman. Hell, just ask Jolene. So he made another attempt to regain control of the conversation. "Anyway, Steve and I have been friends ever since, and as soon as I hit Las Vegas city limits, I usually give him a call. We try our best to find time to at least meet for a drink."

"How long has it been since you've seen him?"

"Too long." Jared had been steering clear of Vegas ever since he'd found out that Jolene had moved back.

The flight attendant announced that it was time for seat backs to be set in an upright position, and Jared was glad to have the interruption in a conversation he hadn't wanted to pursue.

Forty-five minutes later, after landing and picking up a rental car, they arrived at Steve's office, a smoky-glass high-rise located close to city hall. They took the elevator all the way to the top, where Steve's prominent and respected firm took up the entire floor.

Sabrina seemed impressed with the black leather seats, the chrome-and-glass furniture in the reception area. Jared had been, too, when he'd come here the first time.

"We're here to see Steve Rankin," Jared told the young woman seated behind a raised and curved desk that was crafted out of polished cherrywood and boasted a black marble counter.

"I'll let him know you're here. Please, have a seat."

Jared guided Sabrina to one of the sofas, but they didn't wait long.

Steve called his name, and Jared immediately got to his feet and reached out his arm in greeting.

"This is Sabrina Gonzalez," Jared told his friend. "She's my mother's bookkeeper."

As the man and woman shook hands, Jared noticed that Steve held on longer than was necessary, something that suggested the avowed bachelor had found her more than a little attractive.

But how could Jared blame him? Sabrina was a beautiful woman, even when she wasn't in a thin, cotton gown, barefoot and wearing her hair Lady Godiva style.

"Come on back to my office," Steve said, leading the way.

"So what did you find out?" Jared asked. "Are those guys on the up-and-up? And is that offer anything we ought to consider?"

Steve held open the door and indicated that they ought to take the black, tufted leather desk chairs that sat across from his. "Let's just say that you came to the right place."

"What do you mean?"

"Dazzling Desert Ventures is legit. It's the name of an LLC that was created by some big-name casinos. And their offer was relatively fair."

"What does that mean?" Jared asked.

"In terms of the price per square foot, it wasn't too far off the mark." A slow grin stretched across Steve's face. "But let me be the first to tell you that your mama and daddy made one heck of a good investment. That ten acres is worth millions. And since Dazzling Desert Ventures is trying to put together a major deal, and your mother's land is the prime piece, they'll be willing to pay even more."

"How much more?" Jared asked.

"At least twice the amount they offered."

Jared blew out a long, slow whistle. "Looks like we have something to celebrate tonight. Dinner's on me. Champagne, too."

"I'll have to pass. I have a conference call that will take most of the evening. You have no idea how long it took me to line it up, so there's no way I can reschedule it now." Steve leaned back in his chair. "Where are you going?"

Jared hadn't given it much thought. Dinner and champagne had just been a spur of the moment suggestion. He supposed they could go anywhere; most of the top casinos had a nice steakhouse.

So why he answered, "Serenata" was beyond him.

It was one of the most romantic restaurants in all of Las Vegas.

## Chapter Eight

Jared and Sabrina had even more to celebrate than he'd thought.

After Steve had driven them to the property and impressed them with his knowledge of the commercial real-estate market, not just in Clark County, but in all of Nevada, he'd agreed to negotiate the deal as a favor to his friend.

So after checking into rooms at La Trieste, one of the newest and finest casino/hotels on the strip, Jared donned a sports jacket, then took Sabrina to dinner at Serenata, less than a mile away.

Now, as they sat across a linen-draped table from each other, Jared studied Sabrina in the candlelight. She still wore that business suit, which was the dressiest outfit she'd brought, but she'd loosened up and appeared to be more relaxed.

Since their trip was drawing to a close, he wondered if he could get her to let her hair down. Maybe he could suggest going to a show or hitting the casino.

The wine steward arrived at their table sporting a bottle of Cristal, two flutes and an ice bucket. "Your champagne, sir."

"Thank you." Jared watched the man pop the cork and fill the glasses.

"Will there be anything else?" the steward asked.

"No. That's it for now."

The man nodded respectfully, then backed away from their table.

When they were alone, Jared lifted his glass in a toast. The rising bubbles placed a festive mood on the evening. "Here's to a smooth negotiation and to Everett Clayton's foresight when he purchased that desert property."

Sabrina lightly tapped her flute against his, the sound of crystal resonating, then took a sip. "Hmm. I've never had champagne before, but this could become habit-forming. It's really nice."

"This is one of the best, so you have great taste." He tossed her a smile.

"Is it terribly expensive?"

More than she was probably used to spending. "This is a special occasion."

Her lips made a little O, and she nodded. "That means I'll have to save up quite awhile before I have any more."

Sabrina, her blue eyes glistening in the candlelight

and a smile creating dimples, looked like a princess to-night, a woman deserving of all the finest in life.

"What did Mrs. Clayton say when you called her with the news?" she asked.

"She was pleased. But you know, it sounds weird to hear you call her Mrs. Clayton. Almost everyone in Brighton Valley calls her Granny. And the few who don't, call her Edna."

"I don't feel comfortable doing that yet. But maybe someday I will." She took another sip of champagne. "When did you start calling her Granny?"

"Ever since day one."

"When was that?"

Jared didn't usually go in to details with anyone who didn't already know about his early years. But maybe it was the ambiance of Serenata. Or the pretty woman who sat across from him, her smile telling him it was safe to reveal at least some of the past. "I was twelve when Granny threw me a lifeline."

Sabrina leaned toward him, as though they'd reached a level of intimacy. But as the flute listed in her hand, threatening to spill over, he couldn't help wondering if his self-disclosure was also an accident waiting to happen.

"How did she do that?" Sabrina asked.

"She provided me with a home when there wasn't an-other one to be had." Jared was sure that Sabrina could probably relate to that, which was why he continued with the story, sharing what he usually kept close to the vest. "I never knew my mother. And my dad... Well, he had quite a few problems—drugs for one. So when he took off one day and never came back, I was put in foster care."

"Sometimes, when I was growing up, I'd wondered if it might have been better if Carlos and I were taken away from my parents." She took a drink of champagne. "Was being a foster kid a negative experience for you?"

"No one was cruel to me, if that's what you mean." Jared studied his glass, noticing how the candlelight made the bubbling liquid look like a magical elixir. Like a potion that could fix all that had once been wrong in his life and give him a different past. "My first foster father was in the military, and when he received word that he was being transferred to the east coast, he took his family with him, but they had to leave me behind."

"I'm sorry. That must have been tough."

It had been—at the time. But he shrugged it off. "I wasn't a blood relative, so I didn't expect them to take me with them."

"Is that when Granny stepped in?"

"No. After that, I went to live with the Wilsons. They treated me well, and I would have been okay if it had become permanent. But when the parents started having marital problems, counseling hadn't helped, so they threw in the towel and got a divorce."

"And you were uprooted again." It hadn't been a question. Just a conclusion that was easy to come to, especially for a woman who'd experienced a lot of moves herself.

"By the time I hit the teen years, I was placed with a family who got permission to take me to live with them in Brighton Valley. And I finally thought I'd found a place to settle in."

"Was that with Mrs. Clayton?"

"Nope. Hank and Wanda Priestly. But when Hank

developed lung cancer and died, Wanda decided it would be easy on her financially if she moved in with her folks for a while. And their house was pretty small."

Sabrina placed a hand over his, making a connection he wasn't sure what to do with and warming his fingers with hers. Her gentle touch offered a balm—if he wanted one.

He didn't need it, of course. Yet when she removed her hand from his, he wished she hadn't. Still, he continued the story he'd started. "Because of my age at the time, someone at social services decided to send me to the county home for boys."

Jared lifted his glass, savored the taste of the champagne. "Granny has been a longtime friend of Grace Ann Peterson, my foster dad's aunt. So when she heard about me and my plight, she volunteered to take me in even though a social worker said I was a 'rebellious adolescent on the verge of those tumultuous teen years.'"

"Did you give people a hard time?" Sabrina asked. "My brother used to act out a lot when we were growing up. But I always tried to compensate by being good so we wouldn't have to move again."

"Actually, I'd become so distrustful after so many crappy attempts to find a place to fit in, that I'd pretty much given up hope and figured the sooner Granny gave me the boot, the better. So I put on my best surly face and gave her a hard time. But it didn't take long to learn there was something special about Granny. And I soon realized I'd found a home for good. When I was fourteen, she told me she wanted to adopt me, if that was all right with me."

"And obviously," Sabrina said, "it was."

Yeah. It was more than okay. It was the best thing

that had ever happened to him. "It's amazing what a loving mother and a real father figure can do for a kid."

"Did you meet Mr. Clayton? Was he still alive when you went to stay at the Rocking C?"

"No. Clem, Granny's foreman, was a crusty old cowboy who took an instant liking to me and taught me all about horses, cattle and ranching. And for the first time in my life, my future looked happy and bright."

"Clem sounds like a perfect role model for a boy."

Jared couldn't help but laugh. "You've got that right. Clem loved tall tales, good whiskey and five-card stud, and before long, I not only picked up all his good qualities, but most of his vices, too."

"You miss him," she said. "And not just a little. I noticed the way you studied that photograph of the two of you we found in the cabin. And I saw the way you carefully placed it on the mantel."

"You're right. I do miss him. He was unique and a real novelty. They don't make 'em like Clem anymore."

"When did your mother adopt the other boys?"

"First, she took in Greg. Then Matt. But it wasn't easy for me to move over and make room for them. I'd staked my claim and wasn't ready to lose it. So needless to say, there were a few scuffles at first. But we eventually created a family of sorts, something we'd all been missing."

"Did Greg and Matt learn how to play poker and pick up any of Clem's vices?"

Jared chuckled. "Yep. Each in his own way. But since Granny always has been a churchgoing woman and wouldn't have been too happy about our bad habits, we kept them under wraps, believing that what she didn't know wouldn't hurt her."

Sabrina leaned forward again, placing her elbows on the table as though she was finding his tale intriguing. "So how bad were you?"

"Well, I've never been in jail." He flashed her a smile, although she didn't return it.

When Sabrina took another drink of champagne, the steward seemed to appear from out of nowhere to replenish their glasses.

Jared thanked him, and when they were left alone again, he said, "By the time I was twenty-one, I was making regular trips to Las Vegas, where I won at poker and blackjack more often than not. In fact, I was able to put a down payment on a ranch of my own with my winnings."

"So that's what you meant when you said that you'd been to Las Vegas before."

Looking back, probably more than he should have, even though it had given him the financial edge he'd needed to buy his own ranch and become independent. And one trip in particular had been a big mistake—the day he'd met Jolene. Then a few months later, before realizing they weren't the least bit suited, he married her and brought her home to Texas.

They were happy for about a year, but Jared had been busy working his ranch, and Jolene had grown tired and bored.

She left during the holidays—a year ago last November—and it had been especially tough. But rather than rally and join Granny and his brothers in Brighton Valley, Jared chose to drink his way to Groundhog Day.

When Granny learned about the pending divorce and

had revealed her disappointment, Jared had told her they had irreconcilable differences. He was ashamed to let anyone know the truth, that his wife had chosen someone she found more lovable than him.

Jared had been crushed, but in retrospect, he decided it was more from his wife's infidelity and betrayal than by her loss.

"You're a lucky man," Sabrina said.

"I guess I am." Lucky in cards, anyway.

"Mrs. Clayton is a wonderful woman. And you and your brothers were fortunate to have crossed paths with her."

"That's for sure. Granny's love and acceptance were a godsend, although I have a feeling she's the kind of woman who's the exception rather than the rule."

"That sounds like a divorced man talking."

"Maybe so." Jared may have made one mistake, but he wouldn't make another. If he ever got involved with another woman again, he was going be careful about who she was.

One night, after Matt had had the accident and came to live with Jared, the two sat up drinking, commiserating with each other into the wee hours of the morning.

"Jolene was a mistake from the get-go," Matt had said. "That should have been clear to you. But apparently, you don't have a cull shoot when it comes to weeding out the good lovers from the bad. Any fool could have seen that she wasn't the kind of woman a man could trust."

At the time, Jared had gotten hot under the collar, but he'd let it go. Slamming his fist into his crippled brother's nose wouldn't have changed anything.

"Did your mother like your wife?" Sabrina's question came at him like a charging bull, and he didn't quite know how to sidestep it.

"She never said anything negative, although Jolene wasn't very family-oriented."

Thinking Jared was stubborn and a bit on the ornery side, which had probably led to the marital problems, Granny had tried to convince him to go after Jolene, to make his marriage work. But Jared had refused.

"I'm better off now," he told Sabrina, just as he'd told Granny back then. "We both are."

Sabrina offered him a smile. "There'll be someone else someday. Someone better."

"I'm not looking for a replacement."

"Sometimes that's when you find love—when you least expect it."

"And you know that how?"

Sabrina sat back in her seat, taking the glass of champagne with her. "Okay, so I'm not all that experienced with love and marriage. But I do read."

"What do you read? Romances? Self-help books? Articles in women's magazines?" He couldn't help his interest, his curiosity about her take on relationships.

"All of the above, actually."

Romance novels, too? He wondered what she'd learned from them. Or what she thought she'd learned.

"I believe there's someone out there for everyone," she continued. "And you shouldn't settle until the right one comes along."

"You think so, huh?" Jared smiled, thinking her somewhat naive then, signaled for one of the waiters, letting him know it was time to order dinner.

Jared didn't want to keep drinking on an empty stomach. Otherwise, Sabrina's romantic notions might begin to make sense.

For the most part, he'd sworn off women. Not that he wouldn't pursue a sexual relationship now and again. But when he did, he would make sure there weren't any feelings involved or strings attached.

As they waited for the valet to bring Jared's car, Sabrina relished the brisk night air and the clear desert sky. The moon was only a sliver of itself, while the stars winked and blinked as though they were privy to a secret Sabrina didn't know.

She had a buzz from the champagne, but she really didn't care. She and Jared had shared something special this evening. A closeness she hadn't expected.

When she'd first met him, he'd come across as harsh, headstrong and self-righteous. But as the days passed he'd shown her another side of himself—first by reaching out to Joey and giving him a ride on the horse, then by pitching in to help her clean and repair the cabin.

Jared had also gone above and beyond by bringing her wood for the fireplace and making her lunch, all signs of consideration that touched her heart.

And just now, when he shared his past with her, she'd been given a special insight to the man, a glimpse of his childhood that allowed her to understand him in a way others might not be able to.

She suspected there was still a little bit of that abandoned boy inside of him, that child who'd been searching for a place to call home, for a family to love him. It had been an easy conclusion to make, since there was still a bit of the insecure girl in her.

At least he'd found what he'd been looking for.

As she would someday.

A shiver slid over her, and he placed a hand on her back. "Are you cold?"

"Just a little." She offered him a smile, thinking that even though he hadn't actually wrapped an arm around her in a warm, protective sense, his response had been sweet. Affectionate, even.

She wasn't sure what had transpired between them tonight, but after the intimacy of a romantic dinner and the revelations he'd made about his childhood, things had changed.

*They'd* changed. And so had their feelings.

She wasn't exactly sure how, but she felt it in the desert air, in the musky scent of his cologne, in the heat of his palm as it pressed into the small of her back.

As she glanced again at the sky, and the stars that twinkled like magic overhead, a sudden realization struck. If she weren't careful, she could fall for him.

In fact, that just might happen anyway—no matter how hard she tried to avoid it.

As their rental car swung around to the front of the restaurant, one of the valets climbed out and handed Jared the keys, while another opened the passenger door for Sabrina. Moments later, they were headed back to the La Trieste Hotel and Casino.

"Are you up for a little fun?" Jared asked.

Fun? Both the humor in his tone and the gleam in his eyes made the suggestion enticing. "What do you have in mind?"

"Maybe some blackjack?"

"I don't know how to play."

"That doesn't matter. You're a bookkeeper, so you ought to be able to count to twenty-one. Besides, I'm a good teacher."

It was tempting. And she wasn't ready for the night to end. "I really don't have any money I can afford to lose."

"I'll stake you, and we'll split the winnings." He made it sound like a sure thing, but she knew better.

As they pulled into the circular drive and stopped at the entry in front of La Trieste, Jared again left the vehicle with the valet to park. Then he escorted Sabrina inside, where she found herself just as awed by the bright, blinking lights and the blips and bleeps of slot machines as she'd been when they'd checked in earlier today. Maybe more so, now that she realized some of them were paying off, much to the delight of a couple of lucky gamblers.

As they approached an ATM machine, the man turning away and counting the cash he'd just received nodded at Jared in acknowledgment.

"How's it going?" Jared asked, clearly not expecting an answer.

But the man responded anyway. "Not too good, I'm afraid. That's the only machine that's paid off for me all night."

Jared chuckled, then placed an arm around Sabrina's shoulder and guided her through a maze of people and slots.

"You know," she said, as they walked, "I might feel better getting out of this outfit." She still wore her charcoal-gray business suit and heels. "Would you mind if I went up to my room and changed?"

"Not at all." Jared slowed his steps. "I'll just wait for

you in the lounge near the elevators. I might even play one of the poker machines."

"All right. I won't be very long." Sabrina dug into her purse for the card that served as her room key. When she had it in hand, she told him she'd be right back, then strode to the elevator and took it to the twenty-third floor, where they had rooms next to each other.

Once inside, she kicked off her high heels and tossed her purse on the bed. Then she grabbed a pair of jeans and a white cotton blouse from her carry-on bag and took them into the bathroom.

When she'd freshened up and brushed her teeth, she removed her business suit and hung it in the closet. As she closed the mirrored door, she studied her image.

This morning, she'd woven her hair into a neat and professional bun, but the pins had begun to dig into her head. Now she was ready for something less formal. So she let her hair down and brushed it until it shined. Then she swept it into a casual twist, using a silver clip to hold it in place.

She slipped on the jeans. The blouse had gotten a little wrinkly from the trip, but she wasn't going to stress about it. She'd told Jared she wanted to be comfortable, and that was the truth.

Once she'd slid her feet into a pair of sandals, she returned to the casino floor and looked for Jared.

She found him in the lounge, just as he'd promised. He was having a drink and playing a game.

"How'd you do?" she asked, as he cashed out.

He handed her a receipt and grinned. "I did all right."

She glanced at the figure on the paper, seeing that

he'd won over five hundred dollars. "Does this happen to you on every trip?"

"No. But for the most part, I'm luckier than most."

Before they could take a step, a voice sounded behind them.

"Hello, Jared." The soft, feminine tone rang loud and clear.

They both turned, spotting a tall, voluptuous blonde, her face loaded with makeup. Too much, in Sabrina's opinion. But still, the woman was stunning.

"Fancy meeting you here." The blonde, her long, curly hair spritzed and molded into a blowsy style, eyed Jared carefully. "The last I heard, you weren't coming back to this town on a bet."

Jared stiffened for a moment, then seemed to thaw as he slipped an arm around Sabrina's waist, drew her close and introduced her to Jolene.

His ex?

Catching herself and minding her manners, Sabrina extended a hand. "It's nice to meet you."

It wasn't, though. The meeting was completely unexpected and awkward.

"Likewise." Jolene's gaze drifted over Sabrina, as though she was assessing her and finding her lacking.

Was Jared doing the same thing? Comparing the two women?

Jared held on to Sabrina, as if her presence was keeping his demon at bay. The last time he and Jolene had seen each other had been during their divorce proceedings. They'd had words, he'd said something that had ticked her off and she'd flown off the handle, screaming and shouting obscenities.

"It's good to see you," he told her, "but I'm afraid we can't stay and chat. We're headed up to our room."

"Oh… That's too bad." Jolene smiled—one of the fake ones that he'd come to spot a mile away. "I'll have to catch you later."

Not if Jared could help it.

He shouldn't have let her "catch him" the first time.

Jolene might have knocked him on his ass when she told him she didn't love him anymore, that she doubted whether she ever had. And he might have been angry, unbalanced, torn up about it for a while. But in the grand scheme of life, their divorce had only been a minor inconvenience, and he was truly better off without her.

Still, his pride had taken a direct hit.

As he let his hand slide down Sabrina's back, his fingers trailed possessively along her hip. He supposed it wasn't fair to drag her into an emotional pissing contest with his ex-wife, but Sabrina was ten times the woman Jolene was. And as far as Jared was concerned, his ex could eat her heart out.

As he and Sabrina strode toward the elevators, neither of them spoke. To her credit, she didn't mention a word about his ex-wife or the blackjack table they were supposed to be heading toward. Nor had she said anything about the fact he still hadn't removed his hand from the perfect slope of her pretty derriere.

Apparently, she not only sensed his need for escape, but was aiding and abetting him at the same time. And that said a lot about her.

Did she understand that he meant to leave Jolene realizing that what goes around, comes around?

When the elevator opened, they waited for it to empty, then stepped inside. As the door shut, leaving them alone, Sabrina turned, causing his hand to fall from her hip.

She leaned against the wall and crossed her arms. "You lied."

About what? he wondered. The hint of a smile took the edge off her accusation, but he wasn't entirely sure what she was getting at.

Did she mean that he'd lied when he'd said they were heading upstairs instead of the blackjack tables?

Or when he'd implied that they were sharing a hotel room?

He raked a hand through his hair. "I'm sorry about that, Sabrina. But the last time Jolene and I ran into each other, there was a scene. I can never trust her to behave civilly, and I didn't want to embarrass you or myself."

"What are you talking about?"

Had he misinterpreted her question? "You accused me of lying."

Sabrina straightened and crossed her arms, but there was more than a hint of amusement in her eyes. "You made it sound like your ex-wife was an old toad."

"As far as I'm concerned, she is."

"That woman *isn't* fat. And she certainly isn't toothless, unless someone paid for an expensive pair of shiny white dentures."

He snorted. "It's pretty standard in a divorce to see the ugliness inside people." Especially when that someone was caught cheating.

"So you're saying that you have a picture of Jolene stored in your mind, and you mentally blackened a couple of her teeth and drew horns on her?"

"She pretty much added those horns on all by herself." Jared punched in number twenty-three, sending the elevator on an upward path.

"How did she do that?"

He clammed up. It was hard to admit that he hadn't been good enough. That the woman who was supposed to stick by his side for life had found someone she liked better.

And even though he suspected he hadn't really loved her, either, that it had only been a terminal case of lust, he didn't like the betrayal. The cheating.

People who made commitments ought to stick by them.

The elevator came to a stop, and the door opened.

"Come on," he said, leading Sabrina to their rooms.

"Where are we going?" she asked.

His steps slowed.

Where the hell *were* they going? He'd been so intent upon getting away from the sight of Jolene, that he'd concocted the excuse to head upstairs.

Jared raked a hand through his hair—again. "I don't know. Are you up for a movie or something? They've usually got some good pay-per-view options."

"What did she do to you?" Sabrina asked.

His gaze met hers, recognizing the compassion that pooled inside.

Downstairs, he'd pretended that he and Sabrina were lovers. It had merely been a game he'd been playing. But standing outside their rooms, looking in those pretty blue eyes, the game took a turn for real.

Her smile threatened to wring out everything in his heart that the divorce hadn't damaged.

She stroked his cheek, her palm grazing the bristles that had been growing since he'd shaved early this morning. "Not all women are like that, Jared. You've got to let it go."

"I have." And he'd never let it go more than he had this very moment.

"Are you sure?" Her gaze locked on his, demanding the truth and pulling it out of somewhere deep inside him.

All he could see was Sabrina, all he could think about was dusting himself off and climbing back in the saddle again.

"Damn straight, I'm sure." He might be sorry later, but every lick of sense he'd ever had went right out the window as he lowered his head for a kiss.

## Chapter Nine

The kiss began lightly—a brush of the lips. But soon it intensified, and their tongues began to mate, twisting and tasting until Jared thought he might go crazy.

Their hands roamed, seeking and exploring. With each stroke, each caress, their breathing grew more and more ragged.

Still, the kiss continued.

Right there, in the middle of the hallway on the twenty-third floor of La Trieste, Jared found himself making out with Sabrina like a love-struck, hormone-driven teenager.

And he'd be damned if he even cared.

Apparently, neither did she, because she slid her fingers into his hair, drawing his mouth closer, his tongue deeper.

Jared had never lost himself in a woman's embrace before. Not like this. Sabrina was turning him inside out.

She'd claimed that she wasn't all that experienced with this sort of thing, but he found that hard to believe, now more than ever. She kissed like she'd been schooled in the fine art of seduction, and he suspected she had a few things to teach him.

Damn. If they didn't stop this public display of… lust…she'd be giving him those lessons right in a hotel hallway.

He finally broke the kiss long enough to say, "We need to either head back downstairs to the casino or take this inside one of the rooms."

His pulse thudded in his head, and he found himself holding his breath as he awaited her answer.

"I've never done this before," she said, looking a little nervous.

Done what? Necked and made out in the middle of a public hallway? Entered a hotel room with a man?

Pondered having sex for the first time?

If that were the case, it not only pleased him, but added a ton of pressure. If she was a virgin, he'd have to take extra care to make sure it was enjoyable for her. "We'll take things slow and easy. In fact, we don't have to go any further than we've already gone."

Of course, his hormones were shouting, *Oh, yes, we do!*

He reached into the front pocket of his slacks, pulled out the key card to his room and held it up. All she had to do was say the word.

But instead of saying anything, she took the key from his hand and opened the door.

Once inside, he removed the carry-on bag that lay on

the bed, right where he'd left it after they'd checked in, and tossed it onto the floor in the corner. He hoped she didn't think he was making the bed ready for them. He'd just meant to clear off a place to sit down, although neither of them did.

She continued to stand and reached to the side of her head, feeling a loose strand of hair. She undid the clip, but as she began to work the tresses back into a twist, he stopped her.

"Let it hang loose. Please?"

She studied him for a moment, as though she wasn't sure why he'd made the suggestion. Then she combed her fingers through her hair, leaving it long and free.

He caught the strands that lay along her cheek, letting them slip through his fingers like a veil of silk. "I've wanted to do that since the first moment I laid eyes on you."

"I like my hair long," she said. "But it gets in the way sometimes."

"I like it, too."

Desire stretched between them like a tightrope cable ready to snap. And although he knew better than to let things get out of hand, Sabrina had stirred something inside of him that hadn't been tempted in a long, long time. And if things took a sexual turn, he was willing— if she was.

"Like I said, we don't have to do anything you're not ready for."

There. Now the ball was in her court.

Sabrina looked at Jared, at the way his hair had been mussed by her fingers. At the desire that smoldered in his eyes.

She'd turned down opportunities before. And each time, she'd stuck to her guns. But there had been one guy in college who'd made her reconsider. A guy who'd promised she wouldn't be sorry. Since she'd grown increasingly curious over the years, she'd agreed. She'd also insisted that he wear two condoms—just in case.

Jared ran his knuckles along her cheek, and she found herself curious all over again. More so this time because it would be with a man whose kisses sent her to the moon and back.

"So what do you think?" he asked. "Should we hang out here? Or would you rather go downstairs and play a little blackjack?"

She ought to tell him that she wanted to head for the elevators. But she *felt* something for Jared. Something she hadn't anticipated. Something that had her walking a high wire between love and like. And she suspected he was feeling it, too. The only thing holding her back was fear of pregnancy, although she realized she was older now. Wiser. And better prepared for the consequences.

"I don't suppose you have any condoms?" she asked.

"There might be a couple in my shaving kit. At least, I think they're still there."

Well, there went one excuse, leaving them with very few others to consider.

"I'm not completely innocent," she admitted. "But it wasn't… He didn't… Well, I…"

Jared's gaze snagged hers, wrapping her in a cocoon of warmth and understanding, and her heart took a tumble. She was falling for him. She was sure of it.

"Are you telling me the experience was disappointing?" he asked.

She nodded, cheeks warming enough to let her know she was flushing. "I'd read articles about lovemaking and was curious. I also liked the guy, and we seemed to have chemistry."

But not anything like she and Jared had. His musky scent taunted her nearly as badly as the heat of his touch.

"And?"

She cleared her throat, wanting to get the words right. "Well, sex wasn't all that those women's magazines had led me to believe. And I don't think he enjoyed it much better than I did."

"Was it your first time?"

"Yes. And I guess I was expecting too much."

"Maybe." He tossed her a gentle smile, warming her to the bone. "Sex is something that keeps getting better and better."

"Like our kisses?" she asked.

He slid her a crooked grin. "Yeah. Just like that."

"Then if that's the case, I don't think those books and magazines I've been reading are doing sex justice."

"I'd lay money on that." He didn't step any closer; he just opened his arms, allowing the decision to be hers. Yet it hadn't been a difficult one to make.

She slid into his embrace, ready to take things one step at a time, just as he'd told her they would.

He nuzzled her neck, and she turned her head, providing him better access to the soft spot right below her ear. He used his lips and tongue until she feared she would collapse in a molten puddle on the floor. Then he trailed kisses to her mouth, where he assaulted her sweetly, deeply, thoroughly.

A rush of heat swept over her, and she thought she'd die if they didn't finish what they'd started.

He slid his hands along her back and to the slope of her derriere, then he pulled her flush against a demanding erection. She couldn't help but lean into him, yearning for more.

As the heat mounted, she reached up and ran her fingers through his hair again, fisting it, claiming him as her own.

What they were sharing right now, what they were feeling, was more than lust. More than sex. In fact, she feared that the depth and the power of it would change everything—her hopes and dreams.

She couldn't help wondering if, for the first time in her life, the family and stability she'd always wanted were finally within reach.

A groan formed deep in his throat, and he caressed her breasts, his thumbs skimming her hardened nipples and creating an ache deep in her core. Needing to feel his skin against hers, she began to tug his shirttail out of his pants.

In their haste to work together, a button popped off and flew across the room. But they didn't let that stop them. Moments later, they'd removed her blouse and bra, as well.

Jared knew just what to do, where to touch, how to ravish her with his hands. As her nipples contracted in response, her breath caught. But he didn't miss a beat; he just kissed his way from her throat to her breasts, dropping to his knees to do the job right.

Sabrina hadn't been prepared for any of this, not in her past experience, not even in her wildest imagination.

Still, she wanted more and pulled him to his feet. She reached for the button of his jeans, tugging until his hand covered hers.

He drew back, but his gaze, intense and smoldering with heat, never left hers. "Are you sure this is what you want?"

"Yes." She'd never been so sure of anything in her life. She wanted *him.* And she wanted *this.*

She grabbed his waistband again, fumbling for the metal button until he stopped her.

"I'll be right back."

Jared crossed the room in two steps, then dug through his carry-on bag until he found his shaving kit. Sure enough, he found two little packets.

He'd promised to take things slow and easy, but it was a promise he wasn't sure that he could keep. Only a fool could have fought the desire he felt for Sabrina.

She'd admitted to being curious about sex, so he was giving her what she wanted. Yet for a moment, he almost felt guilty. As if he were taking something he didn't deserve.

When he'd protected them both, when they were both naked and wanting, he joined her on the bed and lay claim to all she offered him. Her body was damn near perfect, and he stroked her reverently.

"You're so beautiful," he whispered.

She brushed a strand of hair from his brow, her eyes caressing his face. "When you look at me like that, I can almost believe it."

"There's nothing *almost* about it." He brushed his lips across hers, then trailed kisses from her chin to her breasts. He suckled one nipple and then the other, tasting and taunting her until her breath caught in pleasure.

Yet he was every bit as mesmerized by her touch, by her taste, as she was by him. And when they were both aching with need, he hovered over her.

Her hair was splayed on the pillow case, her blue eyes glazed with desire.

"I want to be inside you," he whispered.

She smiled. "I want that, too."

Then she opened for him and placed her hands on his bare hips, guiding him to where he needed to go, where he needed to be.

He thrust into her. Her fingernails gripped his back, as he began the rhythmic motions.

She lifted her hips, taking more of him, and he increased the tempo. Her breathing—his, too—increased, as they moved in unison, taking and giving. She wrapped her legs around his waist, and as she peaked, she cried out, just as his own climax exploded inside of her.

His eyes were shut, but an amazing display of fireworks shot through his mind, lighting up in a burst of beauty and awe.

Their joining had been better than even he had expected, the kind of lovemaking that lasted all through the night.

Too bad there was only one condom left.

Jared and Sabrina had made love twice last night, limited only by the number of condoms they had.

Now, as dawn broke over Las Vegas and peeked through a gap between the blackout shades, Sabrina lay in the comfort of Jared's arms, her back against his chest, her bottom cradled in his lap.

She'd slept the last couple of hours spooned in his embrace—and not bothered in the least by insomnia.

Never had she imagined loving someone would be like this, both the physical aspect, as well as the emotional. And for the first time in her life, she felt as though she'd found a place where she actually belonged—even though, on the outside, this particular place was just a hotel room.

Because on the inside, where it counted most, she belonged in Jared's arms, in his bed.

In his life.

He stirred, then ran a hand along her hip, possessively. Lovingly.

"Are you awake?" he asked.

"Yes." And still basking in all that they'd shared last night.

"I'd meant to ask you this morning if making love met your expectations, but I don't have to ask."

A smug little smile stretched across her lips. "Why is that?"

"I have the scratches on my back to prove that it was better than you dreamed it would be."

"You're right," she admitted. "And if I didn't have to get back to work and to Joey, I'd be tempted to stay right here and order room service for the rest of the week."

"Speaking of room service…" Jared lifted his head and braced himself on an elbow. "I'm going to order something for breakfast."

Thirty minutes later, they'd showered—together. And what a surprising treat that had turned out to be.

When Sabrina had lamented the fact that they didn't have any more protection until one of them made a trip to the gift shop downstairs, Jared taught her ways they could pleasure each other without the risk of pregnancy.

Interestingly enough, having Jared's baby didn't seem like a scary thought. In fact, she wouldn't mind having a little boy or girl with his eyes, his smile.

Not right away, of course. But someday.

A knock sounded.

"I'll get that." Jared pulled one of the hotel-provided white robes out of the closet and slipped it on. Then he handed the other one to her. "It's probably room service with our breakfast."

After combing out her hair, leaving it wet and long, Sabrina slipped on the robe and joined Jared at the table in the room, where he'd set out a lavish spread. She'd heard him ordering but hadn't paid much attention. Now, seeing it all piled on the table, she was a bit overwhelmed. He'd chosen scrambled eggs, bacon, waffles, fresh fruit, muffins, coffee and fresh-squeezed orange juice.

"Wow," she said. "You must be really hungry."

"I'm used to having a hearty breakfast, but since coming to Granny's, I've been eating pretty light."

"Connie isn't a very good cook," Sabrina said. "But she tries hard."

"What do you know about her? I'm still wondering how that money could have disappeared from Granny's account."

"Not much." Sabrina reached for a piece of toast. "She hasn't been at the ranch very long, and she's pretty quiet. But I really don't think she's dishonest."

"Some of the best thieves can be pretty sly."

"The bank is still investigating but had no news the last time I asked." Sabrina picked up a knife and smeared a dab of butter on her toast. "I'll give them another call when we get back to the ranch."

Yesterday afternoon, they'd decided to let Steve Rankin deal with Wayne Templeton and Dazzling Desert Ventures. Steve had promised to keep them informed via phone, fax and e-mail. They'd also lined up a flight to take them back to Texas later today.

"You know," she said, "after we eat, I'm going to call and check on Joey. I'll let them know we'll be home tonight."

Jared dug into a plate of scrambled eggs, piling his fork high. "That reminds me. Now that you and I have gotten to be…friends, I was wondering if you were going to answer a question I asked you earlier."

"What's that?" She speared a strawberry from the bowl of fruit with her fork and popped it into her mouth. Mmm. So sweet.

"Why did your brother leave Joey with you? You told me he had a good reason, but you wouldn't tell me what it was."

At the time, Sabrina hadn't trusted Jared with Carlos's secret. But they'd reached a new level of intimacy, and it seemed natural to answer any questions he had.

Yet a part of her wanted to keep it to herself—out of shame, out of fear. Things were too perfect between her and Jared right now, and she didn't want to risk ruining it.

But she owed him the truth.

She placed a half-eaten piece of toast on her plate, set aside her pride and decided to trust this man with everything. "Carlos is in prison."

*In prison?*

Jared's fork, which was laden with a scoop of scrambled eggs, hung over his plate. He certainly hadn't expected that answer. "What did he do?"

"He was convicted of assault with a deadly weapon."

Damn. That certainly explained why he was AWOL in Joey's life, but it left Jared feeling uneasy about Sabrina, about her family. And it brought to mind the comment Matt had made. The accusation that bore a ghost of truth.

*Apparently, you don't have a cull shoot when it comes to weeding out the good lovers from the bad. Any fool could have seen that Jolene wasn't the kind of woman a man could trust.*

Had Jared jumped into another physical relationship before learning the true character of the woman he'd slept with?

Instead of beating himself up with the possibility, he focused on her revelation.

"When did he go to prison?" he asked.

"Shortly after Suzy died."

"What provoked the assault?"

"It's probably best if I explain a few things about Carlos to you first. He was young when Joey was born. Only seventeen. And even though he didn't marry Suzy, like I told you before, he got a job so he could support his son. But he was in a Catch-22. With no education or skills, his options were limited. But about a year ago, he lucked out when a national trucking company hired him. And he was thrilled. The pay was decent, and his employer offered health insurance, which was great for Joey. Neither Carlos nor Suzy had been able to provide extras like that in the past, and fortunately, Joey has always been healthy and doesn't need to see a doctor very often."

Jared didn't know anything about kids or their health issues. But Joey didn't have much meat on his bones, and if he ever did get sick, he might have a hard time fighting it off.

Still, Jared understood the importance of health insurance, but a kid needed a dad, too. His own father had abandoned him, and it had taken him a long time to get over the loss and feelings of rejection. Thank God Clem had come along.

But who did Joey have as a male role model?

Trucking was a respectable job, but Jared couldn't help wondering if there was something else her brother could have done for a living. Something that would have enabled him to stay in town and provide for his son.

There had to have been, which is what Jared's mind shouted loud and clear. So for that reason, he didn't share Sabrina's faith in her brother.

Carlos must have enjoyed the vagabond lifestyle, but Jared didn't argue with her. Instead, he waited for her to continue.

"One night, while at a truck stop in Georgia, Carlos witnessed a couple of the locals fighting with another trucker. So he grabbed a baseball bat he kept under the front seat of his rig for protection and tried to scare them off. Things got out of hand, and one of the men charged him. He struck back, and the man was seriously injured."

"That should have been considered self-defense."

"Like I said, they were locals. And they testified that

the other trucker had stolen a wallet from one of them and suggested that Carlos was part of a tag team that had been hitting various truck stops."

"Was he?"

"My brother hasn't always made the best choices. But he wouldn't have been a part of something like that."

Jared wasn't so sure. And he just couldn't find any sympathy for Carlos or his plight. Things just didn't seem to add up.

"What about the other trucker?" Jared asked. "What happened to him?"

"Unfortunately, the police found the stolen wallet on him, so he's in prison, too."

And Carlos had gone to bat—no pun intended—for a thief.

"One of the locals testified that he'd seen Carlos and the other man together earlier, but that wasn't true."

"How do you know?"

"Carlos told me. He tried to explain that in court, too, but neither the judge nor the jury believed him. Now he's serving time in a Georgia prison. I'm hoping that he'll get out in a year or so, but I also hired a private investigator to uncover proof of the lie. So maybe they'll release him sooner."

Private investigators weren't cheap. No wonder she'd had to quit school and go to work. It hadn't been just the day-care situation.

She took a sip of her orange juice, then shrugged. "So there you have it. Now maybe you can understand why I feel so sorry for him. He's gotten a lot of bad breaks in his life."

Jared couldn't buy that. He'd learned that some people just naturally gravitated to the dark side. Carlos was probably one of them, and Sabrina was making excuses for him, which didn't sit right. Her support for the black sheep in her family could only spell trouble, and his uneasy feelings turned to distrust, reinforcing the walls he'd built around his heart, walls Sabrina had been eroding over the past couple of days.

"So what about us?" she asked. "Where do we go from here?"

Was she thinking that they'd shared something more than great sex?

And if so, *had* they?

He'd thought so earlier—before she mentioned that Carlos was in prison. Before he realized that she was offering her brother blind faith and unconditional support, including the cost of a private investigator.

She'd asked him where they were going from here, and he knew she was talking about their relationship. But he really didn't know.

"We're going back to the ranch," he finally responded, his thoughts scampering as he tried to sort through what they'd done, how he felt.

Sure, he was attracted to her. Hell, he was flat-out enamored with her. But he certainly wasn't in a position to make a commitment to her. Nor did he want to set himself up for more heartbreak, more trouble. He just couldn't. Her family situation and her blind support of her brother was too troubling to ignore, even if she was as naive and as sweet as she seemed.

He'd had that kind of faith in someone, too. The kind that convinced a young boy that his father was coming back for him, even when he'd seen the hard evidence of his old man's drug and alcohol addiction, the paternal neglect. And believing in someone who didn't deserve one's faith or love had been a tough lesson to learn.

Heartbreaking, too.

It was bad enough that Sabrina had fallen for her brother's excuses. But she was encouraging Joey to believe in the man's goodness and love, too.

"And *then* what?" she asked, as though probing for a soft spot. For his Achilles' heel.

He found himself weakening for a moment, part of him wanting to throw caution to the wind and see where fate led them. But his logic and defenses won out. The truth was, he didn't know Sabrina very well. For crying out loud, they'd only met days ago.

Hell, maybe she'd been so desperate for money to aid her brother's release from prison that she had embezzled funds from Granny.

It was possible, wasn't it?

There were too many unknowns. He had to think of Granny first.

His own needs, physical or emotional or otherwise, weren't important. He'd come to Granny's ranch to find the thief and needed to get back on track.

"As soon as I return to the ranch, I'm going to find out who's been stealing from my mother. That's why I came to Brighton Valley. And I won't go home until the money is returned and the thief is in jail."

Sabrina stiffened, and he suspected that she'd sensed he'd morphed from a satisfied lover into a suspicious son, a flip-flop that even left him feeling uneasy, awkward and a bit guilty.

As much as he wanted to believe the best about her and completely rule her out as a suspect, succumbing to temptation had left him even more unsettled, more at odds.

Hell, he couldn't trust himself and his feelings right now, let alone Sabrina. And more than that, he just couldn't lay himself bare to betrayal again.

So in spite of what they'd shared, he reached for a familiar defense mechanism and provoked a fight, wanting to do something—*anything*—that would take the heat off him and end a budding relationship he wasn't ready for.

"It could be anyone at the ranch," he said, his gaze targeting her in spite of the lingering uncertainty his heart still felt.

"*Anyone?*"

No. Not *you*, he wanted to say.

But he couldn't allow himself to be sucked into her world, into her unstable family situation. And he couldn't risk having his trust shattered again.

"Yes, *anyone*," he said, his head taking charge of his heart and sending him in for the kill. "Even you."

## Chapter Ten

*It could be anyone,* he'd said.

*Even you.*

Her pulse pounded in her ears, and her temper simmered below the surface, the heat rising until she thought her cheeks might blister.

He'd used her—for sex. His kindness had all been an act—each word, each smile, each touch. Everything that had led up to them making love last night had been an underhanded trick to get what he'd wanted.

Then came the dawn, and Jared Clayton had gone from nice guy to total jerk in zero to sixty milliseconds.

Sabrina wiped her mouth, although there hadn't been any reason to. Then she stood and dropped the linen napkin onto her plate.

If Jared wondered what she was doing, he didn't ask.

She stooped to pick up her clothes and her sandals from the floor where she'd discarded them last night and carried them into the bathroom.

Moments later, she came out fully dressed. Her hair, still wet from their sexy romp in the shower, hung limp and stringy down her back. Under normal circumstances, she would have put some effort into containing it. But there wasn't anything normal about today.

He looked up. A sheepish expression suggested he was going to say something. Apologize maybe, or explain how she'd misunderstood what he'd said and taken it wrong. Yet he did neither, and it wouldn't have helped if he had. He may not realize just how lucky he was that she wasn't throwing things at him.

She patted the front pocket of her jeans, where she'd slipped her key card after leaving her room last night, before running into Jolene and returning upstairs with Jared.

It must have slipped out. Or had she put it in her purse instead?

After a careful search, she came up empty-handed.

"What's the matter?" he asked.

"I'm locked out of my room."

As she headed for the door that led out of the room, he asked, "Where are you going?"

"To the front desk. I'm going to ask for a new key."

He didn't say anything else, which was just as well. He'd shown his true colors.

Once the door snapped shut behind her, the tears she'd been holding back welled in her eyes, and a sense of betrayal clawed at her throat.

She'd known Jared had a suspicious and distrustful side from the first time she'd heard his voice over the telephone line. The night he'd called the ranch asking for Mrs. Clayton and demanding to know who Sabrina was, he'd been rude, which had set her off. But she could almost understand him doing it then, since she'd been a stranger to him, and he was looking out for his mother.

But not now.

How dare he imply that Sabrina might have taken the money? After all they'd shared?

Okay. So it had only been days that they'd known each other. But shouldn't he have seen her true nature?

*Like she'd seen his?* a small voice quizzed.

Truthfully, she'd made her own assumptions about his character, yet hadn't seen the real Jared Clayton until moments ago, when he'd knocked her to her knees with his accusation, his distrust.

She stood before the elevators and waited for one to stop at her floor. She needed to escape—and not just from Las Vegas. She wanted to get as far away from Jared as she possibly could.

Her options were sorely limited, though. But she couldn't continue working at the Rocking C. Not when Jared might show up at any time.

Seeing him again would only serve to remind her of how foolish she'd been. How starry-eyed and gullible.

A bell-like gong alerted her to the arrival of an elevator. Once the door opened and she stepped inside, she pushed *L* for lobby.

She was alone, yet she continued to fight back the tears, watching the numbers overhead through a blur.

On the fourteenth floor, the car stopped for a couple in their fifties. They were wearing shorts, polo shirts and visors.

Were they going to breakfast? Or maybe out to play a round of golf?

"Good morning," the woman said, her voice too cheerful for a time like this.

Sabrina nodded, but found it impossible to speak. How could she pretend that it was indeed going to be a beautiful day when everything inside her screamed that there wasn't anything good or beautiful or nice about it?

On the way down, the couple smiled warmly at each other, which suggested that some people actually found love and happiness, when others never did.

Sabrina averted her eyes, no doubt red and watery and laden with grief.

All she'd ever wanted was to be loved and accepted, to find a place where she belonged. And last night, she'd been swept away by passion and had fantasized that she'd finally found all she'd been praying for.

But she'd been wrong. Jared wasn't the answer to the home and stability she'd dreamed of having. Instead, he'd turned on her.

It was her own fault, she supposed. She'd put her trust in a man who would never trust her.

As the door opened, she stepped into the lobby in front of the couple and stole away from their happily-ever-after glow.

She strode to the front desk, where she had to stand in line for an available clerk. It seemed that all of her life had been spent waiting for something, for someone.

And she was tired of it.

When it was finally her turn, she told the desk clerk that she needed a new key to her room, then provided him with proof of her identity.

"How many do you want?" he asked.

"Just one." And she wouldn't need it long. Just long enough to get her things.

Minutes later, she had access to the hotel room. She'd placed her makeup in the bathroom when she'd first arrived. She considered taking a minute to put on a bit of lipstick and mascara, but opted to find time to do it later. Right now, she wanted to throw her clothes back in her bag. Then she wanted to get out of this hotel, out of this city, out of Jared's life.

He could wrap up that real-estate deal without her. And as soon as she returned to the ranch for Joey, she'd tell Mrs. Clayton that she was sorry, but that she would have to quit—effective immediately.

By the time Jared got back to Brighton Valley, Sabrina and Joey would be long gone.

Minutes later, she was back downstairs. And once outside, she didn't wait for the bellman to call her a cab. She flagged it herself, then climbed into the backseat.

"Where to?" a heavyset man asked.

"To the airport."

He glanced at her through the rearview mirror. "Running late? If so, I can take a short cut and try to get you there faster."

Yes, she was late. She should have left yesterday. Before she'd pinned her heart and her faith on the wrong man.

\* \* \*

Jared sat alone in his hotel room, trying to convince himself that he'd done the right thing. That he'd ended a crippled relationship in the same way he would have put down a horse with a broken leg.

Yet he mourned his actions, too, just as he had when he'd been forced to put his first horse out of its misery. Old Red had died quickly and without lingering pain, but Jared had moped around for days. And this was worse.

He ought to be happy Sabrina was in her own room and that he'd regained control and balance over his life.

But that couldn't be further from the truth. Not when the evidence of their lovemaking surrounded him. The scent of sex, the tangled sheets mingled with the faint whisper of her floral perfume, haunted him with a memory he wasn't likely to ever forget.

And right now he felt more alone than he ever had before.

He picked up a strip of bacon and took a bite, then tossed it back on the plate. The food no longer tasted edible, no longer looked appetizing. Instead, he carried his coffee out onto the patio, noting that the day, cloudy and dark, was just as dismal as his mood.

From inside, his cell phone rang, so he placed his cup on the table and went to look for it. He scanned the room until he could figure out where it was.

It was right where he left it, he realized—in his pants pocket. And his clothes were lying in a heap on the floor.

By the time he located the blasted thing, the call had ended. He pushed the send button and recognized Steve's home number.

After redialing, he waited for his friend to answer.

"Steve? It's Jared. I'm sorry I missed your call, but I couldn't find my phone."

"At this time of day, your cell should have been charging all night and in plain sight. Or did you get distracted after dinner by that beautiful, blue-eyed bookkeeper?"

Jared had been distracted, all right, but he wouldn't admit it. Not when he didn't want to be quizzed about what he'd done—or how he'd chosen to end it. So he steered the conversation back where it belonged. "What's up?"

"I know that I suggested you and Sabrina could head back to Texas today and that we could hammer out the details of our counteroffer later, but Wayne Templeton would like to meet with you while you're still in town. Are you available this afternoon?"

Jared and Sabrina had tickets to fly home this evening, but he could ask her to go on by herself. He'd just extend his stay if he had to. "Sure. I can do that."

After agreeing to meet at Steve's office, Jared disconnected the line, then knocked on the door that separated his room from Sabrina's. Maybe she would be happy to head back to Texas without him.

When she didn't answer, he knocked again. Louder.

Still, no answer.

Thinking she might be in the bathroom, he waited a couple of minutes, then tried the phone. When she didn't pick up, he realized she might not have returned from the front desk.

Did she have a cell? He didn't think so.

Maybe she was avoiding him, and if that was the case, he really couldn't blame her.

If she hadn't taken the money, she'd be deeply offended by his implication. And if she had, then guilt might keep her away.

But was she *really* a suspect? his heart whispered.

The cell phone rang again, and Jared picked it up. Was it Steve calling back? Had there been a change in plans?

A glance at the display told him it was someone from the ranch. He figured Granny was eager to know how the negotiations were going.

He flipped open the cover. "Hello."

"Jared, this is Tori. I'm looking for Sabrina."

"She's not here. I saw her earlier—at breakfast. And I tried her room a while ago, but she didn't answer. She might have gone down to the casino."

"It's important that I find her right away. Can you please look for her?"

Jared stiffened, every fiber of his being going on alert. "Why?"

"I'm taking Joey to the clinic in Brighton Valley, but I have a feeling they'll be sending him to a hospital in Houston."

Jared's gut clenched. Had Joey been injured? Had he gotten kicked or stepped on by Smokey?

There were a million things that could happen if someone hadn't been looking out for the kid.

"What's wrong?" he asked.

"His lips have a bluish tinge, which could mean that he's not getting enough oxygen."

Jared raked a hand through his hair. He remembered the kid trying to catch his breath the day they'd left for Vegas.

"I'm not sure what's going on," Tori said, "but it could mean there's a lung or heart problem."

*Heart?* Sabrina had said his mother had an undiagnosed heart problem. Was it something genetic?

"You go ahead and take him to the clinic," Jared told her. "And let the doctor know that his mother died from a heart attack when she was in her early twenties."

Tori asked for details Jared couldn't provide.

"You'll have to talk to Sabrina about that," he said. "I'll try to find her as soon as possible. Won't you need her permission for him to be treated?"

"Not if the condition is life-threatening."

"Is it?"

"I don't know. But I'll keep you posted."

"Please do." He hung up long enough to call Steve and tell him there was a change in plans.

"Sabrina and I are heading home as soon as possible," he told his friend. Deal or no deal.

When Steve promised to pass along the message to the prospective buyers, Jared hung up the phone, then banged on the door to Sabrina's room again.

Still, no response.

He picked up the phone and called the front desk. Maybe she was still there.

What time was checkout? He glanced at the clock on the bureau. 9:07 a.m. There shouldn't be a line this early. What was keeping her?

"Front desk," a man answered.

"This is Jared Clayton in room 2314. Sabrina Gonzalaz is in room 2316 and went downstairs to get another key to her room, but she hasn't returned yet. Can you let me know if she's still waiting?"

The man put Jared on hold. When he came back on

the line, he said, "I'm sorry, Mr. Clayton. Ms. Gonzalez has already checked out."

Jared's pulse seemed to fade away, and a cold, clammy chill began at his head and shimmied to his knees. "How long ago was that? Is she still in the hotel?"

"I'm not sure, sir. She had a bag with her, but I have no idea where she went from here."

His heart sank to his gut. "I need to check out, too," he told the clerk. "Use the credit card I have on file and mail the receipt. I'll leave my key in the room."

Jared dressed quickly and threw his belongings into his bag.

Where had she gone?

To another hotel?

Not likely.

To the airport? Hoping to get an earlier flight out? That was his best and only guess.

Fear twisted a knot in his chest, as he hurried out of the hotel and hailed a cab.

He had to find her before she got on board an airplane. If she headed to the ranch instead of to the medical center, where Tori said they would most likely be sent, it would take hours longer for her to get to Joey's side.

A kid needed his mother at a time like this.

And Sabrina was the closet thing Joey had to one.


"Attention please," a crackly voice called through an airport paging system. "Sabrina Gonzalez, please pick up the white courtesy phone."

Sabrina sat up straight and keened her ears. It sounded

as though her name had been announced, but she wasn't sure if she'd heard correctly. Then the message repeated, and she realized someone was looking for her.

She'd told two different airline representatives that she'd like to go standby on their next flights to Houston. Maybe one of them had found her a seat.

Hopeful, she scanned the gate area until she spotted a white, wall-mounted phone.

There was one. By the ladies' restroom.

She hurried to answer the page. "This is Sabrina Gonzalez. I was asked to call."

"Yes," a male voice said. "Ma'am, there's a gentleman in the airport looking for you. He says his name is Jared Clayton, and that it's an emergency."

Jared had come to the airport looking for her?

Was he feeling remorse about the things he'd said, the implications he made? Was he having second thoughts?

Maybe he figured that his apology qualified as an emergency, but she didn't. Not that she wouldn't want to hear what he had to say.

She supposed it wouldn't hurt to give him a moment or two of her time, but that wasn't going to change anything. She wasn't staying in Las Vegas one moment longer than she had to. And she would even leave Brighton Valley as soon as she could pull it off.

Sabrina clutched the receiver until her knuckles ached, reluctant to make this easy for him, yet wanting to get it over with so she could be on her way. "Tell him I'm sitting between gates C-three and C-four."

She hung up the phone and returned to her seat. She doubted there was much Jared would be able to tell her that would make any difference. He'd shown her what kind of man he was. And when it came to seeking a mate, she was looking for so much more than that.

A glance at her wristwatch told her she might want to check again with the customer-service rep at Wild Blue Air. He'd been working behind the desk at gate three had had suggested that she check back with him about the availability of seats on Flight 419. Apparently, there'd been a delay in San Francisco, and it didn't look as though some of the passengers would make their Las Vegas connection to Houston.

She stood, and just as she reached for her bag, she noticed Jared striding toward her. Not wanting to give him the satisfaction of thinking she was waiting with bated breath to talk to him, she looked the other way, focused on the planes that were parked at the gates.

Yet curiosity got the better of her, and she stole another peek.

His hair was tousled as though he'd left the hotel in a rush.

Is that because he was eager to apologize and set things right?

The closer he got to where she stood, the clearer she was able to see his expression—intense, determined…

Maybe she'd been wrong. Maybe what he had to say might matter after all—at least a little. Still, it wouldn't be easy to forgive him for not trusting her.

Yet as he drew near, she realized the expression he wore was more than remorse.

It was grief. And…fear?

As much as she wanted to turn her back, to avert her gaze again, she knew something was wrong.

Terribly wrong.

"Tori called," he said.

She tightened her grip on her bag, her heart pounding as though it might burst. "Did something happen to Joey?"

"Yes. Tori thinks there could be a problem with his heart or lungs. And she's taking him to see Doc Graham in Brighton Valley."

Ringing and buzzing swirled in her ears as she tried to sort through what he was telling her. "Why didn't she call me?"

"Did you bring your cell phone with you?"

"Yes."

"Then it must be turned off. I tried to call you, too." He handed her his. "Her number is the top one, so just hit Send twice."

She did as he instructed, but got no answer. Rather than push End, she waited long enough to leave a voice mail message. "Tori, it's Sabrina. Jared found me. I'm at the airport already and heading home. Please call me as soon as you can. I'm worried sick."

"Try the ranch," Jared suggested.

When she did, Connie answered.

"What happened?" Sabrina asked. "What's going on?"

"Earlier this morning, Joey was out in the barn. Apparently, one of the cats had a litter of kittens. He was so excited, he hurried in to tell Tori and me. But when he got inside the house, he could hardly breathe. And Tori immediately sensed something was wrong."

"Did she say what?"

"No. She didn't want to scare him and make it worse." Connie blew out a sigh. "You can't believe how good she was with him, soothing him and calming him down. Anyway, she and Granny took him to see Doc Graham. She thinks it might be his heart."

"His *heart?*" Sabrina could almost feel the color leave her face. "Oh, my God. No."

"I haven't heard anything more, but Tori wanted me to give you her cell number in case you called in."

"Thanks, I have it. And moments ago, I tried to call her, but she didn't answer."

"Maybe they're in with the doctor."

That was certainly possible. She remembered that there'd been signs posted at the hospital where Suzy had been taken. The use of cell phones was prohibited in some places because it interfered with the medical equipment.

"If Tori calls you," Sabrina said, "will you please tell her that I'm trying to get a flight home as quickly as possible. All she needs to do is let me know where to meet her."

"I'll sit by the phone," Connie said.

Sabrina disconnected the line, then handed the cell back to Jared.

He took it, slipping it onto a clip on his belt, then slid an arm around her. "I'm sorry, Sabrina."

About *what?* His ploy to wangle a sexual romp? His distrust?

Or was that all water under the bridge? Was he trying to pretend that none of it had happened and that the two of them had somehow become good friends? That he actually cared about her and about Joey's health?

"What can I do to help?" he asked.

*Nothing,* she wanted to say. *Not a damn thing. Just*

*leave me alone. Let me stand on my own two feet and take care of my nephew.*

But she'd never been one to play tit for tat.

"If you had a hotline to God, that might help. If you had a medical degree… If…" A tear slipped down her cheek, and she swiped it away.

"I can't imagine how tough this is for you."

He was right; he couldn't.

"I don't want you to have to go through this alone," he added.

What was he saying? What was he offering?

He hadn't even apologized for believing the worst about her, so if she accepted his support, how long would it last?

"The only one who would be of any help right now is my brother," she said, a bit of a snap to her tone. "And unless you can spring him from prison, then I'm going to have to face this on my own."

"Where is he?" Jared asked, as though her response hadn't been spoken with an ounce of sarcasm, anger or frustration.

"Grayson State Prison. It's in Georgia."

Jared reached for his cell and dialed a number. When the line connected, he introduced himself and asked to speak to Steve Rankin. Moments later, his friend apparently answered.

"I need to talk to a good criminal-defense attorney," Jared said. "Do you have someone you can refer me to?"

Sabrina couldn't hear what Steve was saying on the other line, but she listened to Jared's side of the conversation.

"I didn't do anything," he said. "And no, that's not why I cancelled today's meeting. The referral isn't for me. Sabrina's brother, Carlos Gonzalez, got into some trouble a while back and is incarcerated in Georgia. His young son may be seriously ill, and I want to see if there's anything that can be done to get him some kind of furlough—if the boy's condition turns out to be life-threatening."

When Jared disconnected the line, he turned to Sabrina. "Steve is going to make a few calls and then get back to me."

She didn't dare put any hope into Jared's attempt to help. But she did appreciate the thought and thanked him.

"You're welcome. Have you managed to get an earlier flight home?"

"I'm still working on it." She glanced at her watch, seeing that it was time for her to check in with the airline again. "I put in several requests. And there's a possibility I can catch the eleven-o'clock flight out on Wild Blue. The man I spoke to thought he might be able to give me a better answer after ten o'clock."

"I'll see if they can find a seat for me on that flight, too."

Sabrina wanted to tell him not to bother, to go ahead and stay in Vegas for whatever meeting he'd scheduled, but she didn't care what he did.

Not anymore.

As she turned to make her way to the desk, Jared followed behind.

She supposed he was just trying to be supportive, but at this point, she didn't care. Last night, she'd thought she'd fallen in love with him, but this morning she'd learned the man she'd once believed him to be didn't exist. And when he'd implied she was a thief, she'd lost whatever trust she'd placed in him.

When it was her turn at the counter, she addressed the airline representative. "Is there an update on my request for a seat on flight 417?"

"You're in luck," the man said.

She hoped so. Lately, it seemed that the cards had been stacked against her.

## Chapter Eleven

Just before boarding the plane, Jared's cell phone rang. Sabrina waited long enough to realize it wasn't Tori, then proceeded through the gate.

While she followed the other passengers, she again tried to call Tori, using the number Connie had given her. Once the flight was underway, she wouldn't be able to use her cell.

This time, thank goodness, the call was answered. The background noise at the airport made it difficult to hear, though, so Sabrina covered one ear with her hand and pressed the phone tightly against the other. "Hi, Tori. It's me, Sabrina. What's going on? I've been trying to reach you."

"I'm sorry. We were in the clinic, and I had to turn off my phone."

"How's Joey?" Sabrina asked.

"He's doing okay. He's a great kid."

She blew out the breath she'd been holding and whispered a silent prayer of thanks—short and to the point. "So he'll be all right?"

"Joey's sitting next to me. I'll let you talk to him in a minute. But we're on our way to Houston to visit a friend of Doc's. His name is Dr. Pantera, and he's a cardiologist. In fact, Doc is making the arrangements for us, so all we have to do is walk right in and tell the other doctor that we're there to see him."

It didn't take Sabrina long to realize that Tori was being cryptic on purpose, that she was trying not to frighten Joey. "Is his condition serious then?"

*"Yes."*

Every cell in Sabrina's body seemed to implode, and it was all she could do to gather her wits and try to make sense of the news.

"How did you pick up on the problem?" she asked.

Tori didn't respond.

"Oh," Sabrina said, "you can't really tell me right now, can you?"

"No, I'd rather not." Tori cleared her throat, then her tone suddenly grew chipper, worry-free. "And do you know what? Granny told us we'd really like Doc Graham, and she was right. He's the nicest doctor I've ever met. And you may not know this, but I used to be a nurse."

"So because of your medical background, you picked up on something I missed?"

"Yes. And before I pass the phone on to Joey, I was hoping you might be able to fill me in on his medical history."

"You mean, the condition that led to his mother's death?"

"Exactly."

"I don't have all the particulars, but her doctor's name was Jaime Ramirez. He has an office on Westheimer. The cardiologist should be able to get the information needed."

"Great. I'll take it from there. We'll be in Houston before you know it."

"I'm headed that way, too."

"Call me as soon as you land. Now, if you'll hold on a second, I'll pass the phone to Joey."

When Joey's voice answered, Sabrina tried to duplicate the same upbeat, nothing-to-be-worried-about tone that Tori had been using. "Hey, buddy. Have you missed me?"

"Uh-huh."

She paused, trying to think of something to say. Something normal. Something that would hide her panic, her aching heart. "Connie told me that one of the barn cats had kittens."

"Yeah. And you should see them, Sabrina. They're really cute."

"Why don't I ask Granny if she'll let us have one."

"Really? No kidding?" Just the enthusiasm in his voice seemed to make him breathe a little harder. Why hadn't she noticed before?

Or was his condition worsening?

She feigned a happy tone, all the while battling tears. "Sure, I'd love to have a cat. They're small and easy to care for. And we'd never have to worry about mice. I probably haven't told you how much I hate those little critters."

"I love the ranch," he said. "First I get to take care

of a horse, and now I get to have my very own kitten. I think I'll pick the little black-and-white one. He's the littlest one, but he's so cute."

"Great." Sabrina cleared the wobbly word from her throat. "Can I please talk to Tori again?"

"Okay."

Moments later, when Tori was back on the line, Sabrina asked, "I'm sure Doc looked at Joey as a favor to Granny. But will the cardiologist treat him without my consent?"

"I'm sure he'll want it—even if it's just a verbal okay since you're en route. But there are times when they don't have to follow protocol."

"You mean, when it's considered a serious emergency?"

"Yes, if it's…extreme."

"Are you trying to say that my consent won't be necessary if this is life-threatening?"

"Yes, but I'm not sure if that's really the case. At least not right now."

Sabrina gripped the cell phone as though that somehow gave her a better handle on all that was happening, on all that could go wrong. "Then you don't think Joey's condition constitutes an imminent emergency?"

"I'm not sure. There are other…modes of transportation, and Doc didn't suggest one."

Like an ambulance? Or a Life Flight helicopter?

"Why don't you call the cardiologist?"

Tori must have passed the phone to Granny, because the older woman asked, "Are you ready? I'll give you the number."

Sabrina tried to talk herself out of crying as she dug

through her purse for a pen and a scrap of paper. "Yes. Go ahead." As soon as Sabrina had the number, she disconnected the line, then dialed Dr. Oliver Pantera's office before the flight attendants could tell her to turn off the cell.

She explained who she was and provided the necessary information regarding Joey's medical insurance. Thank God she'd gone with her gut feelings and made the COBRA payments to continue Joey's coverage after Carlos was incarcerated and lost his job. It had been an expense she hadn't really been able to afford, but it appeared to have been a wise decision now.

Jared, who'd waited in the gate area to finish his own call, was now sliding into the seat beside her. "What did Tori say?"

"Not as much as I would have liked her to. With Joey sitting next to her, it was hard for her to go into any real detail. But it's serious. Dr. Graham sent them to a specialist in Houston."

He reached for her hand, and she threaded her fingers through his before realizing she hadn't wanted his solace or even his presence. Yet something deep inside her craved it anyway.

"Tori seems to know quite a bit about illness and injuries," Jared said.

"She used to be a nurse."

"But not any longer?"

"Apparently not."

"Why is that?"

The anger and heartache Sabrina had been harboring, as well as fear about what was happening to Joey, came crashing down upon her, and what little control she'd mustered over the past hour dissipated. She turned to him and snapped. "Dammit, Jared. Just let it go, will you? For *now?*"

He gave her hand a gentle squeeze, warming it and providing a moment of comfort. "I didn't mean to upset you. I was just curious, that's all."

She unlocked her fingers and pulled her hand away. "Just because you don't know anything about a person doesn't mean they're a criminal or worse. Tori has been very nice to me, very accepting. And she's been good to Joey, too. I don't care what her story is. Nor do I give a rip if she has a motive to steal. She's shown her true colors to me—just as *you* have."

Jared didn't say a word in his defense, although Sabrina wasn't sure if that was to his credit or not. But the words had been said, tossed down like a gauntlet.

Neither one of them picked it up, though, which was fortunate. Sabrina really wasn't up for a fight.

Not until she found out what she was up against in Houston.

Jared was in one hell of a fix. And to be honest, at least with himself, he was also running scared.

Of course, at thirty thousand feet above the ground, he wasn't going anywhere too quick.

Seeing Sabrina worried and hurting caused something inside him to melt, to collapse.

His pride, maybe? His fear of making the same mistake twice?

Either way, she sure had him walking a fine line. Part of him wanted to skedaddle, while the other was determined to stick by her side.

The fact that they'd made love last night had sure complicated things and probably contributed to that "should I stay or should I go?" dilemma he was facing now.

Then again, that really wasn't a decision he was free to make. Not after he'd had that knee-jerk reaction to her question about where their relationship was heading.

All right, in retrospect he wasn't entirely sure that he'd made the right decision to end things this morning. But at this point, he wasn't ready to do anything differently.

They really hadn't known each other very long—just a few days. And he'd yet to decide if he could trust her. Then, when she mentioned her brother being in prison, he'd panicked and decided to cut bait and run.

So what was he doing here with her now, when he had every excuse to remain in Vegas for a business meeting?

He was just trying to…

Well, he didn't actually know what he was attempting to do. Supporting her through Joey's illness, he supposed.

And maybe, at the same time, appeasing his conscience for not being a more considerate lover, at least after they'd climbed out of the shower, bright-eyed and sexually sated.

He'd said he was sorry, though. But he hadn't been clear about what. And he still wasn't sure.

Apologies had never come easy for him. And while he really didn't believe that Sabrina could have taken money from Granny, he wasn't ready to backpedal or try and reverse the direction their relationship had gone.

Damn. The woman had him straddling fences.

But he *would* stick by her for a while. At least until

she got back to Houston and faced whatever it was that Joey was going through.

He figured that was the least he could do.

In spite of all he tried to tell himself, he *did* have feelings for her. And he certainly could understand why she'd been upset with him about what he'd said earlier, about what he'd implied.

For that reason, he'd decided to leave her alone, keep quiet and let her cool off. Maybe she would come to the conclusion that Jared wasn't a jerk, even if he might have behaved like one earlier today.

The flight had been airborne for nearly two hours, when he finally decided that she'd had enough time to cool down, that they could talk without her wanting to bite his head off, although he really couldn't blame her if she did so again. His comments and implied accusation had certainly doused the embers of a warm afterglow following a night of lovemaking he would never forget.

So, hoping to make things right, he tapped her arm with his. "I meant to tell you earlier, but it slipped my mind."

"What's that?"

"Right before boarding, I talked to Darrell Schwartz, one of Steve's colleagues. I told him about Carlos, and he's going to research the case and see if there's anything he can do to get him out of prison, if there's any reason to appeal. And if you'll give me the name and number of the private investigator you hired, I'll pass it on to him. He's also going to contact your brother's attorney in Georgia, so he'll need that information, too."

"Why…?" Her brow furrowed. "I mean, I appreciate your help, but why would you do that?"

Because he owed it to her?

Because he wanted to help in any way he could?

Because he'd come to care for her?

He didn't want that to be true, but he was afraid she might have sucked him into something that he was helpless to fight off, something he was too afraid to think about, let alone admit.

Instead, he said, "I'd like to be your friend. And I want to help you because your brother means a lot to you."

Apparently, she bought his explanation because she reached into her purse, pulled out the P.I.'s business card and handed it to him. "I can't help with the attorney, though. Carlos used a public defender, and I'm not sure who he was."

"I'm sure Darrell has a way of finding out."

She nodded, then bit down on her bottom lip and snared him with those pretty blue eyes. "Do you think he'd be able to get a message to Carlos faster than I can?"

"Let's wait to hear what the cardiologist says first." Jared hadn't meant to imply the two of them were any kind of team. But the suggestive pronoun had rolled off his tongue anyway—just as if they hadn't ended things.

"You're right," she said, skipping right over the "*we*." "I really don't want to cause Carlos any undue worry. He's been through so much in his life already."

"You've mentioned that more than once," Jared said. "Are you talking about Suzy's death, as well as the assault charges and the prison term?"

Or had there been more to it than that, as she'd implied?

Jared wasn't sure why he'd quizzed her about it, why he'd even broached the subject of her brother when she seemed to be so touchy about the guy. But a part of him wondered if maybe she'd been right. Maybe there were things Jared didn't know, things that would make him understand and sympathize—as unlikely as that seemed.

"Carlos is a great guy, and if you met him, I think you'd like him. But he had a tough childhood and more than his share of struggles."

"I imagine you both did."

She picked up the glass of diet soda one of the flight attendants had passed out earlier and took a sip. "My brother's problems were a lot worse than mine. He'd had some health issues growing up, as well as attention deficit disorder. No one understood all that entailed, so it seemed as though he was always getting into trouble for one thing or another. And most of the time it hadn't been his fault. At least, not intentionally."

Jared didn't say anything. He just let her talk, realizing how much he'd missed the soft lilt of her voice, especially when it wasn't marred by the snappy tone she'd been tossing his way ever since he'd implied she was a suspect in the theft of Granny's money.

That possibility, he now realized, seemed more and more unlikely with each passing minute.

"Carlos also had learning disabilities as a kid, so schoolwork was a real struggle for him. Then, on top of that, because we had to move so many times, he and I changed schools a lot, too. The poor kid never could seem to get caught up in class. I remember him crying and begging my mom to let him stay home. And a lot of times she'd give in and let him, just to make it easier on her and whomever we were living with at the time."

"What about you?" Jared asked. "Did you hate school, too?"

"No, I enjoyed getting out of the house. And the work was easy for me. The constant moving was tough, though. But I guess I was more adaptable than my brother."

"Did that affect your relationship with him?"

"In what way?"

"I figure it might have been tough for a guy to compete academically with a bright sister who was able to roll with the punches and who kept bouncing back."

She shook her head. "I don't think so. I never detected any jealousy or resentment. Carlos and I were very close growing up. We looked out for each other. We really had to. No one else paid much attention to us or our needs. In fact, we weren't rewarded for good grades or punished for not doing well in school. It just didn't seem to matter. Everyone was too busy living their own lives." She glanced out the window, her gaze searching the fields below that spread out like a giant patchwork quilt.

"So when Carlos had to drop out of high school to support Suzy and the baby," Jared said, still trying to get a grip on Sabrina's family history, "I imagine he was probably glad to have a reason to quit."

"Yes, in some ways. But he knew the lack of education would always hold him back, too. He never could seem to find a job that paid more than minimum wage. And what made it worse was that he could barely read. Whenever I tried to tutor him, he'd get really frustrated. But never more than when he turned eighteen and tried to take his driving test. The poor guy failed time and again."

"How'd he become a trucker?"

"A couple of years ago, I learned that the Department of Public Safety had a program for disabled people that provided alternate testing methods. In my brother's case, he was allowed to have someone read the questions to him. And that time he made a perfect score."

No wonder she was so sympathetic toward her twin. They'd become a team growing up, parenting each other and becoming a family in and of themselves.

At least, that's the way it seemed to Jared, now that he understood what their lives had been like.

"Carlos would do anything for me," Sabrina added. "And I hate not being able to help him right now."

"You're watching Joey for him while he's in prison."

"Yes, but I would have done that anyway. Joey's a sweet little boy, and I love him." She grew silent for a moment, then added, "By the way, Carlos told me that he enrolled in a prison-sponsored literacy program. He said that he was finally catching on and making some progress. He even mentioned the possibility of getting a GED."

"That's good." But it didn't solve her brother's immediate problem: Joey's heart condition could be very serious.

Sabrina looked out the window again, this time closing her eyes.

"Are you okay?" Jared asked.

She turned, her gaze wistful and teary. "I have to be. That child needs me."

It was true. And Jared realized she intended to be there for the boy through thick and thin. Just as she'd always been for her brother.

His stubborn heart quivered and threatened to

melt, which was too damn bad. Sabrina might never forgive him for what he'd said to her in the hotel room this morning.

And if she didn't Jared could suffer his biggest loss yet.

The moment the plane touched down, Sabrina turned on her cell and called Tori for an update.

The onetime nurse answered on the third ring.

"Hey," Sabrina said, as she walked out of the plane and into a hallway that led to the airport. "We're in Houston now. What's going on?"

"They've taken Joey in for an echocardiogram."

"What's that?"

"It's a test in which an ultrasound is used to examine the heart. It allows the doctor to see a cross-sectional slice while it's beating. They'll be able to check out the chambers, valves and major vessels to see what's going on inside and to determine the best way to treat it."

"And what, exactly, *is* the problem?" Sabrina asked, glad that Tori was away from Joey and could explain and answer all the questions she'd been having.

"When we took Joey into Brighton Valley, Doc picked up a serious heart murmur, which is why he sent us to Houston to see Dr. Pantera. And, of course, Doc was right."

Tori had been the first one to pick up on the problem, and Sabrina realized she hadn't taken any credit for that. She would thank her in person, of course, but right now, she was still trying to understand all she could about Joey's ailment.

"Is this something that just developed?" Sabrina asked. "I don't remember him ever having trouble breathing before. And he never complained about anything feeling weird or hurting."

"Dr. Pantera explained that children with Joey's condition are usually in normal health and don't have any symptoms at all, other than a heart murmur. But in Joey's case, there's a serious obstruction to the blood flow between the left ventricle and the aorta. And while rare, there are documented cases where it was the cause of sudden death during strenuous sports activities."

Like his mother's heart attack while jogging.

"Suzy never mentioned him having a heart murmur," Sabrina said. "Or any health problems at all."

"It's possible that the condition worsened over time. When was his last physical?"

"I have no idea. I'm not even sure who his pediatrician was. Or if he even had one." Sabrina grimaced, hoping she hadn't neglected to do something that could have prevented this. She'd scrimped and gone without so that she could pay for his insurance benefits, but hadn't taken him in for an exam. Of course, she'd only had him a few months....

"The tests they're running will tell Dr. Pantera exactly what's going on and how he can treat it."

Jared, who was walking beside her now, slid an arm around her and guided her through the airport, following the throng of people heading for baggage claim and on to their destination. And as much as she wanted to lean into him, to accept his strength and his presence, she knew better than to depend on him for anything at all.

She and Joey were in this alone.

"So it's correctable?" Sabrina asked, holding her breath.

"Hopefully. We'll know more after they finish running all the tests."

"Okay." Sabrina blew out a sigh. "I'll get to the hospital as soon as I can. We only have carry-on luggage, so it won't be long. Where can I find you?"

"We're in a waiting room near the cardiac wing."

Sabrina thanked her, then disconnected the line. Maybe she wasn't all alone after all. Tori had been a godsend, and so had Granny.

She glanced at Jared, who'd now ushered her outside and toward the parking garage.

"Do you mind giving me a ride to the hospital?" she asked.

He looked at her as though she had a giant cuckoo bird perched on her head. "Of course, I don't mind. And I'm going with you. I plan to stay until we find out what's wrong with Joey."

*We?*

She knew better than to read anything into his statement. He had, after all, grown close to the boy, going so far as to give him a horseback ride around the ranch and promising to give him lessons when they returned from Las Vegas.

But Joey wouldn't be getting any lessons anytime soon.

And Sabrina and Jared were a long way from becoming a "we."

## Chapter Twelve

Just before four o'clock, Sabrina entered Whitman Memorial Hospital with Jared at her side. He seemed to know just where he was going, and she let him lead the way.

As he took her past the information desk and straight to the elevators, she finally asked, "Have you been here before?"

"Yes. Hank Priestly, my foster dad, stayed here a couple of times before he died. Wanda used to bring me and their kids to visit, and sometimes I'd feel like a fifth wheel. So I'd say I had to find a bathroom, then I'd slip out and roam the halls, checking out the place."

She tried to think of Jared as a young boy, as a kid who hadn't quite fit in—just as she hadn't when she'd been a girl.

"I know you're in a hurry to see Joey," he said, "but if you'd like a tour later, there's a pretty cool broom closet I can show you on the fifth floor and a stairwell on the sixth that has a great echo. All you have to do is say the word."

She glanced up at him, and even though they continued on their way at the same pace, their gazes locked and something warm and fluid passed between them. She ought to hate him, to etch his distrust in stone on her mind, but during Joey's crisis, she appreciated his presence, his attempt at support.

He tossed her a boyish smile that turned her heart on end, and she realized he wasn't really offering her a tour; he was just trying to lighten things up, to make her feel better.

"It sounds like a fabulous adventure," she told him, "so I'll keep it in mind."

He escorted her to the elevator, and when the doors slid open, they stepped inside. Then he pushed the button that would take them to the second floor.

His musky scent, fading as the day wore on, permeated the air she breathed, causing her to want to take another whiff, to lean against him and absorb some of his strength. But she couldn't trust him to offer that support forever. And that was that kind of loyalty and commitment she would require from him.

Ever since learning of Joey's medical condition, he'd been especially thoughtful. Yet she realized his kindness was merely an outpouring of concern for the child he'd grown to care for. It had nothing to do with her, with *them*.

Still, as much as she wanted to remain at odds with the rugged rancher, that was growing more and more difficult to do with each passing moment.

Falling out of love with him, she feared, wasn't nearly as easy as falling in love had been.

The door opened, and they took a left, following the corridor.

"You really do know your way around this place," she said.

"Yep. It seems like only yesterday when I was a twelve-year-old explorer trying to avoid adult detection." He tossed her another heart-thumping, boyish grin. "But since we haven't reached our destination yet, I'd better not gloat."

Their soles clicked along the squeaky-clean linoleum until he slowed in front of a waiting area just off the cardiac unit. The small room with pale blue walls and connecting brown tweed chairs was nearly empty, except for a middle-aged couple and Sabrina's silver-haired employer.

Mrs. Clayton stood as they entered, then offered Sabrina a warm embrace. "How are you holding up, dear?"

"All right." Thanks in part to Jared, she ought to add, but she wasn't ready to admit it. "How's Joey doing?"

"He's fine. And not the least bit worried. Everyone's been very nice to him, especially Tori."

"She used to be a nurse," Sabrina added, as though it all made perfect sense.

"Yes, I know."

Mrs. Clayton didn't explain, and Sabrina didn't question her. Interestingly enough, Jared didn't jump on that tidbit of information, either, like he'd done on the plane. Maybe he was afraid she'd snap at him again.

Should she credit him for that?

Maybe, but there still hadn't been an apology or any remorse.

"Tori's with Joey now," Mrs. Clayton said. "I thought it would be best if I waited here until you two arrived."

Good. Sabrina didn't want Joey to be alone or scared.

Granny arched her back and stretched, as though trying to work out a crick. "You know, Tori is going to make a wonderful wife and mother someday."

"I'm sure you're right," Sabrina said. "I really appreciate her taking such a personal interest in Joey. In fact, you've both been wonderful. I don't know how to thank you."

"There's no need for that. Joey is a precious little boy, and I can't imagine being anywhere else." Mrs. Clayton again took her seat. "From what I understand, they've run all the necessary tests. And we're just waiting for the cardiologist to come in. Doc says he's tops in his field."

"Maybe I should find Joey and let him know that I'm here now."

"That's a good idea," Mrs. Clayton said.

But before Sabrina could make a move, a man in a white lab coat poked his head into the room. "Ms. Gonzalez?"

Sabrina stiffened and turned to face him. "Yes?"

"I'm Dr. Pantera."

She joined him instantly.

The doctor, a slight man with dark hair and compelling brown eyes, reached out to shake hands and introduced himself as the cardiologist. "Joey has a condition that causes obstruction to the blood flow between the left ventricle and the aorta."

"It sounds serious."

"Yes, it can be. I talked to Dr. Ramirez, the attending physician who treated his mother in the E.R. before her death, and it appears that the condition is genetic. I realize you've just become Joey's guardian, but I suspect he hasn't been seeing a doctor for regular checkups. If he had, the heart murmur would have been picked up during a routine physical. It's the kind of murmur that would have been followed up on, even by someone who wasn't a cardiac specialist."

Sabrina couldn't remember Suzy mentioning anything about Joey having a pediatrician, just that it had been a blessing that he'd been exceptionally healthy.

"Will he need open-heart surgery?" she asked, her stomach clenching at the thought.

"No. We should be able to do a balloon dilation through cardiac catheterization."

"Is that dangerous?"

Dr. Pantera placed a hand on Sabrina's shoulder. "There's always some risk, and I know how frightening all of this is to parents and guardians. But we've made tremendous strides in these treatments over the years. Sometimes we do them as an outpatient procedure, although I'd like to keep Joey overnight, just as a precaution."

Knowing he wouldn't have to stay in the hospital for days made her feel slightly better. "And the procedure will correct the problem? Permanently?"

"Well, it won't correct the valve itself, which sometimes needs to be replaced with a donor valve or an artificial model. But it does decrease the obstruction from severe to mild in a large majority of the patients."

"When will you do it?"

"Actually, we may be able to do it later tonight. I'll let you know for sure in a few minutes. In the meantime, you can see Joey now. He's been asking about you."

"Can I come, too?" Jared asked.

"Certainly." Dr. Pantera led them into the cardiac unit, along with Mrs. Clayton, then asked a nurse to take them to Joey's room, where he lay in bed, the TV set on the Discovery Channel, the volume turned down low.

Tori, who'd been seated in a rocker near the boy's bed, stood when they entered.

"Hey," Sabrina said, as she approached Joey. "I leave for one day, and look at you lounging around and reaping all kinds of attention."

Joey grinned. "Cool, huh? And this bed goes up and down. All I have to do is push this button."

"That's pretty fancy," Sabrina said.

"I told Granny that you said we could have the little black-and-white kitten," Joey said.

Sabrina was about to remind him that he shouldn't refer to her employer as Granny, but decided to let it ride. They had been through a lot today, and the formality no longer seemed all that important.

Joey, who'd been resting his back against the raised mattress, shot up straight and looked at the elderly woman. "And if it's okay with Sabrina, I can have the little orange one, too. Right?"

"As far as I'm concerned," Granny said, "you can have the entire litter as soon as you get out of here."

"Oh, no," Sabrina said. "One little cat will do."

"But with two, they won't get lonely," Joey countered. "And they can catch more mice."

"What a deal." Jared chuckled. "I can tell you from experience that you don't want to be within ten feet of your aunt Sabrina when she sees a rat or a mouse. You'll be holding your ears while laughing your head off."

"Hey!" Sabrina bumped his arm with hers, as though she didn't want to be the butt of a male joke. But in reality, she was happy to see Joey smiling, to know that—God willing—he would pull through and not suffer the same fate his mother had.

Dr. Pantera entered the room. "Well, we're in luck. I've got things lined up, and we can take Joey in for the procedure shortly."

It all seemed to go quickly, although Sabrina suspected it was more like an hour or so. Someone from pediatrics came in with a puppet and explained things to Joey in a way that made him feel comfortable with what was about to happen.

"When it's all over," Jared said, "and I get a chance to talk to Dr. Pantera, I'll ask him about those horseback-riding lessons I'm going to give you and find out how soon we can start them."

Joey grinned. "Cool."

Sabrina had yet to tell anyone she planned to quit working for Granny, that she and Joey would be moving, but she supposed that would have to wait until Joey had recovered.

And until he'd received at least one riding lesson. She suspected he'd never forgive her if she put the kibosh on that.

After they wheeled Joey out of the room, Tori suggested they head to the cafeteria for a bite, and Jared, of course, led the way.

Even though Sabrina hadn't eaten anything since breakfast, she didn't have much of an appetite.

She was too worried about Joey and how he would fare.

Once in line at the cafeteria, Jared followed Sabrina, noticing that while she looked at each selection, she neglected to put anything on her tray.

"What's the matter?" he asked. "You've got to be hungry."

"I know, but at the same time, nothing really looks that good to me."

Jared picked up a bowl of fruit and placed it on her tray. "Try this." Then he stopped by the sandwiches. "Turkey, beef or ham?"

"Will you split it with me?" she asked.

No, he wanted a thick, juicy burger, although he figured they'd give him one of the healthy versions here. But she didn't need to know that. Nor did she need to finish whatever sandwich she picked. Just a couple of bites would do. Something to keep her stomach from growling and to provide some nourishment.

So he told her he'd share, hoping that would convince her to take the whole thing, even if she only wanted half.

"How about turkey?" he asked.

When she nodded, he placed a plastic-wrapped sandwich on her tray.

They neared the cash register, where a middle-aged brunette was totaling the items Tori and Granny had chosen.

Jared pulled out his wallet and addressed the cashier. "I'll get all of this."

"You don't have to do that," Sabrina protested. "I can pay for my own."

"I know that I don't *have* to. But I want to."

After he paid the tab and accepted the unnecessary appreciation of all three women, he joined them at a table in the rear of the cafeteria. They sat near a window that overlooked the grounds. In the distance, the city lights sparkled, providing evidence that the rest of the world were going on with their lives while Jared and Sabrina struggled with their own problems. And not just because of what Joey was going through right now.

They had a relationship that needed mending, although he wasn't quite sure exactly how to go about it. Or when it would be appropriate.

Jared chose the seat next to Sabrina, but she merely studied her food.

Tori reached across the table and placed her hand over the top of Sabrina's. "I know how hard this must be for you, but Dr. Pantera has an excellent reputation. I'm sure everything will go well. We need to be thankful that the problem was diagnosed before we found out the hard way."

Sabrina blew out a soft sigh. "I know."

Tori's comments seemed to ease Jared's worries, too, and he wondered again what the pretty redhead's story was, where she'd come from.

He knew better than to ask, though. No way would he risk upsetting Sabrina, who was pedaling as fast as she could to stay on top emotionally.

All he wanted to do was to see her smile again. To

catch that glimmer in those pretty blue eyes and know they were sparkling just for him.

He stole a glance at her, watched as she took her fork and poked at a strawberry in her bowl of fruit. She lifted it, but didn't put it into her mouth.

"You know," she said to everyone at the table, "I really need to tell Carlos what's going on. Do you think they'd let me talk to him if I called the prison?" She glanced first at Tori, then at Granny.

Her gaze finally landed upon Jared, as though he were the last word on the matter—the one who had all the answers.

At one time, he'd thought that he had. But Sabrina had him tossing aside his well-worn, know-it-all attitude and convinced that he needed to stop and think things through. To smell the roses…

Or rather, in her case, the hint of the floral scent of her shampoo.

"If it would make you feel better," he said, "you could call the prison and ask what the protocol is. Then, if they'll let you get a message to him, you can leave one that's upbeat. You know, like, 'Good news. We picked up on a problem with Joey's heart, and the doctors are correcting it now. I'll keep you posted.'"

"That's a great idea, Jared. I can tell him without making him worry too much." The relief that flooded her face turned his heart topsy-turvy and made him feel like some kind of hero.

Damn, that was nice.

He was glad that he'd finally done something to please her. Something to set things right. But he knew it wasn't going to be enough.

She popped the strawberry into her mouth, then placed the fork back on the tray. Taking her purse into her lap, she dug through it until she found her cell phone. "She dialed information and waited for a bit. Then a grimace stretched across her face. "I'm not getting any reception here. I'm going to go outside and try again."

As Sabrina strode out of the cafeteria, Jared watched her go. Ever since learning of Joey's condition, he'd stayed by her side. He'd tried to offer his support, even though at times she seemed to look right through him.

There was no reason for him to hang out and wait, but he couldn't leave.

He was concerned about Joey, of course, but it was more than that. If Sabrina needed a shoulder to lean on, he wanted it to be his.

Tori lifted her soda, and the lid shifted, splattering cola down the front of her white T-shirt. "Darn. Would you look at that? I'd better try and wash this before it stains."

When she excused herself, Jared watched her walk toward the ladies' room, leaving him and Granny alone.

With both young women out of hearing range, he couldn't help pursuing his curiosity. "Do you have any idea why Tori gave up nursing?"

Granny picked up her napkin and blotted her mouth. "She mentioned something to me while we were waiting for them to run one of Joey's tests, but I think she ought to be the one to talk to you about it."

"Then maybe I ought to ask her."

"No. Under the circumstances, I think you should wait and let her tell you when she's ready."

Which might be never, Jared realized, and that only

made him all the more curious. Before he could conjure another question that would provide a hint, his cell phone rang.

When he answered, a woman sniffled on the other end. "Jared?"

"Yes?"

"It's Connie." Her voice sounded waterlogged, as though she'd been crying or was suffering from allergies. "How's Joey?"

Damn. He should have called her to keep her posted. "The doctor is performing some kind of procedure he expects will clear up the problem. And if all goes well, they'll discharge him tomorrow."

"Good," she said. "Will you be coming back to the ranch tonight?"

He doubted Sabrina would want to leave Joey at the hospital. Something told him she'd be staying, which meant that he'd be here for the duration, too. "I'm not sure yet. Tori and Granny will probably be heading home tonight. Sabrina is outside trying to talk to her brother. When I see her, I'll ask her to give you a call."

"Okay, thanks." Connie released a wobbly breath. "I'm glad he's doing okay. He's a neat kid."

"Yes, he is." Jared had no more than disconnected the line when his cell rang again.

"Hey," Matt said. "How's Joey doing?"

"I think he's going to be all right. We hope to talk to the doctor soon and will know more then."

"Good."

Silence.

When there was no attempt on Matt's part to end the call, Jared asked, "Is everything okay at home?"

Matt grumbled, then swore under his breath.

"What happened?"

More silence.

Finally, Matt let out a heavy—guilt-riddled?—sigh. "I snapped at Connie, hoping to make her angry so she'd leave me alone, but I didn't realize she was so damn sensitive."

Jared knew the cook was pregnant, which probably didn't help.

"God," Matt said, "I *hate* it when women cry."

"Have you been drinking?"

"Some. Why?"

"You can be a real jerk sometimes, Matt. Especially when you're commiserating with a bottle of Jack Daniel's."

More of the damned silence stretched across the line, which made Jared realize his assumption had hit the mark.

"I'll let you go," Matt said. "I'm going to bed."

"That's probably just as well. Your apology might mean more to Connie in the morning."

"You mean, if I'm sober?" Matt swore under his breath. "Maybe you ought to mind your own business."

Determined to not argue with a man who'd been drinking, Jared disconnected the line.

"Is there a problem at the ranch?" Granny asked.

Jared didn't want to upset his mother, so he said, "Nothing out of the usual."

Tori, who was sporting a wet splotch on her white blouse, returned to the table and took a seat beside Granny. "What was that all about?"

"Matt's been grieving," Granny said. "And he's been

drinking, which can make him thoughtless. I don't really know the details, since Jared clammed up, but I think Matt made Connie cry."

Jared hadn't realized she'd put two and two together so quickly.

"Is he an alcoholic?" Tori asked.

"No, although he's been drinking more these past few months than usual." Granny opened a packet of ketchup and squeezed it onto her paper plate, right beside a pile of golden-brown French fries. "He was the driver in a fatal car accident. His fiancée and her son were killed, so he carries a lot of guilt. There's also a question about whether he'll walk again."

At this point, Jared wasn't sure if Matt really cared if he'd get up out of that wheelchair or not. If so, he would have gone back to physical therapy, like he was supposed to.

"How sad." Compassion splashed across Tori's face. "That poor man. Maybe I should talk to him."

"I wish you would," Granny said, as if she believed Tori had some kind of magic potion that would make Matt jump out of his wheelchair and be the man he once was.

Jared knew better, though. But it wasn't his place to discuss his brother's past or future with a stranger, no matter how good Tori had been to Sabrina and Joey.

"I have an idea." Granny dipped the tip of a long fry into the ketchup. "Maybe you can talk him into helping you plan a surprise birthday party for me. I'll be eighty next month."

"I love parties and would be happy to organize it," Tori said, "but we can't call it a surprise if you already know about it."

"I don't see why not." Granny popped the fry into her mouth and ate it. "Each year there's a couple of folks who put their heads together and try to plan a surprise for me, but then someone always spills the beans."

Tori chuckled and a grin tugged at Jared's lips. Granny was right. She'd done so much for so many in Brighton Valley that people just naturally wanted to do something nice for her.

But the subject of the party dissipated in the air, as Sabrina returned and took her place at the table.

"Any luck?" Jared asked.

"I was able to talk to Carlos for a few minutes and told him I'd call back later and let him know what Dr. Pantera had to say." She took a couple of bites of her sandwich, but then set it down and grabbed her napkin. "I'm eager to get back to the waiting room in case the doctor comes looking for me. I don't want to miss him."

"I'll go with you," Jared said.

They strode along the corridor to the elevator, arms brushing against each other. He felt compelled to take her hand in his or to slip his arm around her and draw her close, yet did neither.

As far as being a couple or a team, he'd shot himself in the foot this morning. Now, as the day progressed to night, he'd become more and more aware of how wrong he'd been about her.

When the elevator door opened, they stepped in, joining an older woman and a dark-haired teenage girl. No one spoke until the next stop, which was his and Sabrina's.

Jared took her arm and led her to the waiting room. It seemed as though his whole life—or at least the future—rode on whatever happened next.

"I need to tell you something," he said.

"What's that?"

"I realize you didn't take Granny's money, that you wouldn't have done something like that."

Her steps slowed, and she turned to face him, her gaze snaring his. "What changed your mind?"

*You did.*

*What we shared last night.*

*What you've been revealing to me about yourself over the past few days.*

"I was a jerk," he said. "And I'm sorry. Will you accept my apology?"

She looked at him for a moment, those sky-blue eyes searching for something. Sincerity, he supposed.

"All right," she said. "I forgive you."

Was it enough? Did he need to say more?

Before he could think of a response, a voice sounded from the doorway. "Ms. Gonzalez?"

They both turned to find Dr. Pantera entering the room. A smile broke across his face. "Joey's doing just fine. In fact, his condition wasn't as serious as I'd anticipated, and the procedure went better than expected. We'll keep an eye on him, but I see no reason why he can't go home sometime tomorrow."

"Oh, thank God." Sabrina grabbed the side of the nearest chair to steady herself.

"We'll take him into recovery for a while, and someone will let you know when you can see him. In the meantime, do you have any questions?"

"He's really going to be all right?" Sabrina asked.

"Yes. There will be some limitations, but nothing that will hamper him growing up to be a happy, healthy adult."

Sabrina blew out a soft sigh, and Jared slipped an arm around her. They'd become a team in all of this, and it felt good. Right.

They both watched as the cardiologist left the room.

"That's great news," Jared said.

"Yes, it is. I can't wait to tell my brother."

"I'm sure he's been worried. And when you make that call, tell him I've got an attorney trying to get him released."

"Thanks, Jared. I appreciate that. And Carlos will, too."

Of course, the poor guy would probably go back to driving a truck, which was fine. But Joey needed more of his time, especially while he was recovering from surgery. Too bad her brother couldn't find something...

"You know," Jared said, "why don't you tell him that once he's out of prison, I have a job for him on my ranch—if he wants it. And there will be a place for Joey, too."

Her lips parted, and her eyes glistened as she searched his face. "Why are you making that kind of offer?"

"Because I've come to admire you. And if you tell me your brother is a decent guy and conscientious, I believe you."

"He *is*. And I appreciate your faith in him." She turned, facing him full-on.

"It's *you* that I have faith in, Sabrina. And I'll go to bat for Carlos because I believe in you."

"Does that mean you trust me without question?"

Days ago, he might have had doubts about believing in people in general. But not *her*. Not any longer. The only thing she'd stolen was his heart. "Yes, I trust you."

She smiled and brushed a kiss on his cheek.

His heart swelled, and his lips quirked in a crooked grin. Yet for a moment, the little boy who lived deep within him, the child who'd been deserted, protested.

Jared had jumped into a relationship with Jolene before getting a chance to know her. And look where that had gotten him.

But Sabrina wasn't like Jolene. She didn't ditch her commitments or abandon loved ones—not Carlos, not Joey. And if she had a lover or a husband, Jared realized, she was the kind of woman who would vow to love a man until death parted them, and she'd stick it out, no matter what—even during the bad times.

Unlike Jolene.

After his divorce, Jared had vowed not to get involved with another woman for a long, long time—if ever.

But that was before he'd met Sabrina, a woman who was sure to bring out the best in him, if he'd let her.

And he had every intention of doing just that.

"This morning I made one of the biggest mistakes I've ever made, and I can't tell you how sorry I am. I want another chance. I want our relationship to grow."

She studied him for a moment, her lips parted, her eyes searching his for signs of deceit. But she wouldn't find it.

"I can't see how this will work, Jared. With you living a hundred miles away, we'd be hard-pressed to be anything more than lovers. And I want more. A lot more. The next time I sleep with a man, I'll be laying my heart on the line. And I'm not going to risk doing it with someone who won't take that same risk."

"What makes you think I wouldn't be doing that, too?"

"Would you?" she asked.

Jared raked his hand through his hair. "I've been burned before, and I damn sure don't want to make another mistake. And that makes this scary for me because I'm feeling so much more for you than I ever felt for Jolene."

"How much more?" she asked, a grin putting a sparkle in her eyes.

"I could fall head over spurs in love with you, if I haven't done so already."

A tear slipped down Sabrina's cheek, then another.

He brushed them away with his thumbs. "What's the matter? Am I screwing up again, saying all the wrong things?"

"No. You're saying all the right things." Then she wrapped her arms around him and lifted her lips to his.

They shared a promise-filled kiss that dazed him with wonder. And when it ended, they stood in the middle of the hospital waiting room, holding on to all they'd found—a chance at love and the home they'd both been wanting.

"Why, there you are," Granny's voice said from the doorway, drawing their attention from each other.

Seeing that Granny was alone, Sabrina asked, "Where's Tori?"

"Just as I was getting into the elevator, she got a phone call and said she'd meet me up here." Granny's grin broke into a full-on smile. "But this is a lovely surprise."

*"This?"* Jared asked, afraid he knew what she was getting at.

"I had a feeling that you two would make a good match."

"You *did?*" Sabrina asked.

"Well, I was *hoping* you would. That's why I sent you both to Vegas. I thought you'd find out you had something in common besides looking out for my best interests." Granny crossed her arms and shifted her weight to one foot. "And if either of you had told me that property was worth one dime less that five million dollars, I would have insisted that you sit tight and wait for me to get there and square those casino bigwigs away myself."

"You knew the value of that property all along?" Jared asked.

"Of course, I did. You don't think I fell off a turnip truck, do you?"

"Actually, I *was* a little worried. But I'm happy to find out you're just as ornery and cagey as ever."

Granny laughed.

Moments later, Tori joined them, and Sabrina filled them in on the news Dr. Pantera had just announced.

Granny blew out a huge sigh of relief. "Oh, thank goodness."

"By the way," Tori said to Granny, "that was Connie who called me a few minutes ago. She said someone from the Brighton Valley Savings and Loan came out to the ranch looking for you. One of their tellers was arrested for pilfering funds from elderly account holders, and you were one of them."

"Why steal from senior citizens?" Granny asked.

"Apparently, the teller carefully selected older account holders he thought would be less likely to catch on to what he was doing."

"Well, shame on him," Granny said.

Jared had a few choice comments he could make

about the thief, but he held most of them back. "I hope he gets all that's coming to him and more."

"Me, too," Granny said, yawning. "Boy, oh, boy. This has certainly been a long day. But I'm glad everything has worked out well."

"So am I," Tori said. "But we'd better go. We've got a long drive back to the ranch."

"You're right, and I'm winding down fast." Granny looked at Sabrina, then at Jared. "I suppose I don't need to worry about you two finding your way home."

"Nope." Jared slid his arm around Sabrina and held her close. Not when home was where the heart was.

"Give Joey our best," Granny said, as she and Tori turned to go. "We'll see you all tomorrow."

As they left, Jared turned to Sabrina. "Now, where was I?"

"In my arms," she said, "and in my heart."

"You got that right." Then he drew her close and kissed her.

There was no telling how they'd work this out, but Jared didn't care.

Love would find a way—one sweet day at a time.

* * * * *

*Don't miss Tori and Matt's story,*
*IN LOVE WITH THE BRONC RIDER*
*The second book in Judy Duarte's new miniseries*
**A TEXAS HOMECOMING**
*On sale June 2008,*
*wherever Silhouette Books are sold.*

*Enjoy a sneak preview of*
*MATCHMAKING WITH A MISSION*
*by B.J. Daniels,*
*part of the*
**WHITEHORSE, MONTANA** *miniseries.*
*Available from Harlequin Intrigue in April 2008.*

*Nate Dempsey has returned to Whitehorse to uncover the truth about his past...*

Nate sensed someone watching the house and looked out in surprise to see a woman astride a paint horse just on the other side of the fence. He quickly stepped back from the filthy second-floor window, although he doubted she could have seen him. Only a little of the June sun pierced the dirty glass to glow on the dust-coated floor at his feet as he waited a few heartbeats before he looked out again.

The place was so isolated he hadn't expected to see another soul. Like the front yard, the dirt road was waist-high with weeds. When he'd broken the lock on the back door, he'd had to kick aside a pile of rotten leaves that had blown in from last fall.

As he sneaked a look, he saw that she was still there, staring at the house in a way that unnerved him. He shielded his eyes from the glare of the sun off the dirty window and studied her, taking in her head of long blond hair that feathered out in the breeze from under her Western straw hat.

She wore a tan canvas jacket, jeans and boots. But it was the way she sat astride the brown-and-white horse that nudged the memory.

He felt a chill as he realized he'd seen her before. In that very spot. She'd been just a kid then. A kid on a pretty paint horse. Not this one—the markings were different. Anyway, it couldn't have been the same horse, considering the last time he had seen her was more than twenty years ago. That horse would be dead by now.

His mind argued it probably wasn't even the same girl. But he knew better. It was the way she sat the horse, so at home in a saddle and secure in her world on the other side of that fence.

To the boy he'd been, she and her horse had represented freedom, a freedom he'd known he would never have—even after he escaped this house.

Nate saw her shift in the saddle, and for a moment he feared she planned to dismount and come toward the house. With Ellis Harper in his grave, there would be little to keep her away.

To his relief, she reined her horse around and rode back the way she'd come.

As he watched her ride away, he thought about the way she'd stared at the house—today and years ago.

While the smartest thing she could do was to stay clear of this house, he had a feeling she'd be back.

Finding out her name should prove easy, since he figured she must live close by. As for her interest in Harper House… He would just have to make sure it didn't become a problem.

* * * * *

*Be sure to look for*
*MATCHMAKING WITH A MISSION*
*and other suspenseful Harlequin Intrigue stories,*
*available in April wherever books are sold.*

## Silhouette®

# SPECIAL EDITION™

*Introducing a brand-new miniseries*

# Men of Mercy Medical

Gabe Thorne moved to Las Vegas to open a
new branch of his booming construction
business—and escape from a recent tragedy.
But when his teenage sister showed up pregnant
on his doorstep, he really had his hands full.
Luckily, in turning to Dr. Rebecca Hamilton for
the medical care his sister needed, he found
a cure for himself....

**Starting with**

# THE MILLIONAIRE AND THE M.D.

## by *TERESA SOUTHWICK,*

*available in April wherever books are sold.*

# REQUEST YOUR FREE BOOKS!

## 2 FREE NOVELS PLUS 2 FREE GIFTS!

*Silhouette*®

# SPECIAL EDITION®

### Life, Love and Family!

**YES!** Please send me 2 FREE Silhouette Speäal Edition® novels and my 2 FREE gifts (gifts are worth about $10). After receiving them, if I don't wish to receive any more books, I can return the shipping statement marked "cancel." If I don't cancel, I will receive 6 brand-new novels every month and be billed just $4.24 per book in the U.S. or $4.99 per book in Canada, plus 25¢ shipping and handling per book and applicable taxes, if any*. That's a savings of at least 15% off the cover price! I understand that accepting the 2 free books and gifts places me under no obligation to buy anything. I can always return a shipment and cancel at any time. Even if I never buy another book from Silhouette, the two free books and gifts are mine to keep forever.

235 SDN EEYU   335 SDN EEY6

Name _____ (PLEASE PRINT) _____

Address _____ Apt. # _____

City _____ State/Prov. _____ Zip/Postal Code _____

Signature (if under 18, a parent or guardian must sign) _____

Mail to the **Silhouette Reader Service:**
**IN U.S.A.:** P.O. Box 1867, Buffalo, NY 14240-1867
**IN CANADA:** P.O. Box 609, Fort Erie, Ontario  L2A 5X3

Not valid to current subscribers of Silhouette Speäal Edition books.

**Want to try two free books from another line?**
**Call 1-800-873-8635 or visit www.morefreebooks.com.**

* Terms and prices subject to change without notice. N.Y. residents add applicable sales tax. Canadian residents will be charged applicable provinäal taxes and GST. This offer is limited to one order per household. All orders subject to approval. Credit or debit balances in a customer's account(s) may be offset by any other outstanding balance owed by or to the customer. Please allow 4 to 6 weeks for delivery. Offer available while quantities last.

**Your Privacy:** Silhouette is committed to protecting your privacy. Our Privacy Policy is available online at www.eHarlequin.com or upon request from the Reader Service. From time to time we make our lists of customers available to reputable third parties who may have a product or service of interest to you. If you would prefer we not share your name and address, please check here. ☐

SSE08

**SAVE $1.00**

Family crises, old flames
and returning home…
Hannah Matthews and
Luke Stevens discover that
sometimes the unexpected
is just what it takes to start
over…and to heal the heart.

# SHERRYL WOODS

New York Times BESTSELLING AUTHOR

**SHERRYL WOODS**

*Seaview Inn*

"Flesh-and-blood characters,
terrific dialogue and substantial stakes…"
—*Publishers Weekly* on *A Slice of Heaven*

*On sale March 2008!*

---

**SAVE $1.00**

**on the purchase price
of SEAVIEW INN
by Sherryl Woods.**

Offer valid from March 1, 2008, to May 31, 2008.
Redeemable at participating retail outlets. Limit one coupon per purchase.

52608272

5 65373 00076 2 (8100) 0 11475

® and TM are trademarks owned and used by the trademark owner and/or its licensee.
© 2008 Harlequin Enterprises Limited

MSW2529CPN